*The Whys
and Wherefores
of Littabelle Lee*

The Whys
and Wherefores
of Littabelle Lee

Vera and Bill Cleaver

ATHENEUM 1973 NEW YORK

To B. Blaine Pennington

Copyright © 1973 by Vera and Bill Cleaver
All rights reserved
Library of Congress catalog card number 72-86929
ISBN 0-689-30080-8
Published simultaneously in Canada by
McClelland & Stewart, Ltd.
Manufactured in the United States of America by
H. Wolff, New York
Designed by Harriett Barton
First Printing February 1973
Second Printing August 1973

*The Whys
and Wherefores
of Littabelle Lee*

CHAPTER ONE

When was it all of this took place? Oh, not so long ago, and yet long ago, when I was sixteen and had not yet learned to take notice of time. I heard no knell for the departed months and years; there were so many ahead. I had not discovered everything in myself or yet even half of it. What was there to discover? When a person, simple and childlike in nature, looks in his mirror, he doesn't expect to see the image of a great thinker look back. And a good thing too.

Until I turned sixteen, I went to school during the fall and winter months and sat at a desk, learning a few facts about the world. In the summers I was a sweet roamer. Sometimes I would go with my Aunt Sorrow to the woods to gather medicine plants or ride into the back hills with her to see after a patient; she was a nature doctor.

We lived then, as we live now, in the Ozark Mountains with the old, unspoiled hills rising up all around us and the hollows and watered valleys a part of our everyday scenery. The western plains are near, and because the two old grandparents who abide with me here know only their own geography and live on the garnerings of earlier years, they think the buffalo still range the prairie that lies westward. Paw Paw Lee, whose age depends upon his mood, lays claim to the memory of this state as it was before the turn of the century when it was still a frontier. He can spin some yarns concerning those days. He is a true Ozarker, slow of movement and action, respectful of our superstitions and religions, loyal to family and this land. This land is wound around his heart and he will never leave it. Maw Maw is a little copy of Paw Paw.

It used to be Aunt Sorrow was not far behind my grandfather when it came to telling a big windy. She related the tale of Jean Ladeau, a Frenchman with a desperate reputation, who roved the mountains and valley streams with a band of Quapaw Indians. One day while skinning a deer he plunged a rusty knife into his palm and developed blood poisoning. His Indian friends left him on the trail to die but Jean found his way to the Lee cabin and Aunt Sorrow, who was then just beginning her career as a nature physician, bedded him down in an out-building, covering him with a layer of blankets, then one of straw, then another of blankets and so on until there was a pile two feet thick. Through this she poured near-to-boiling water to which had been added pounds of mineral salts and hay chaffings. Jean steamed like a pudding. She dosed him with two of her vulneraries—a fresh plant tincture brewed from purple cone flowers and another medicine coming from a low, shrubby plant of one of the relatives of the Saint-John's-wort family. For several days poor Jean was given nothing to swallow except raw, fresh goat's milk with a little honey in it. After his fever went down and the poisons had begun to drain, he was fed dried sunflower seeds, raw vegetables, sun-dried fruits, natural rolled oats and fish. Aunt Sorrow said he was not her favorite patient. He complained with every breath and before he had regained all of his health got away from her. Saddled up one night while she was sleeping and rode off to look for his Indian friends. He found them encamped on the bank of the Rumpus River, all down with a liver disease. He died among them from this illness.

Aunt Sorrow said, "I wouldn'ta cared about him dyin' so much if he hadn'ta come to me with his first two miseries, expectin' me to save him. I did and that's the thanks I got for my trouble. He sneaked off from me and died anyway. Seemed like he was just determined."

Jean Ladeau was not Aunt Sorrow's only disappointment. She wanted to go away to school and learn to be a real doctor with proper credentials but could not. There was never enough money.

Like his English and Scottish forebears, all of whom

were peasant yeomen, Paw Paw always lived hard by this land. Aunt Sorrow said she doubted he ever made more than four hundred dollars in any one year from his crops and livestock. He and Maw Maw married while they were still mere children and then their children started to come, Aunt Sorrow first, then my uncle Hutchens, then Aunt Estie and Aunt Ora. And then my father, whose given name was Camus. I never knew him—my father—or my mother. They drowned in the Rumpus River when I was an infant. When this happened, Hutchens, Estie and Ora geared up their few personal belongings and ran off down the mountain to become town dwellers. Like the Frenchman in Aunt Sorrow's windy, I complained too much and they just could not see having to share their already overcrowded quarters with a squalling infant. Aunt Sorrow said all three pitched first-class fits the day I arrived:

"As if we didn't have our hands full enough. It had been rainin' a straight, solid ten days and the rapids just up above us here was beginning to sound like kettledrums. The Rumpus rose at least ten feet and part of the banks on the other side of it slid down into it. All the animals was scramblin' to higher ground. We couldn't think what Camus and his wife was thinkin' about in tryin' to cross over to this side with a baby not yet six months old. You know how wide and tricky the Rumpus is. It didn't get its name for nothing. But to get back to the day you came to live with us, I remember it clear as any commonplace, the whole thing. There was so much mud and water, and all Camus and his wife had to carry

them across from the other side of the river was a little
flat raft. Paw Paw and Maw Maw and I had got out early
that morning. One of our cows had got loose, and we
went down toward the river lookin' for it. The sun was
up, and I remember how pretty it was shinin' on all that
water and the way the little woodpeckers and peewees
and thrushers sounded. They were glad for the sun and
to be alive. Hutchens and Ora and Estie was in back of
Paw Paw and Maw Maw and me. We thought we saw
the cow and we went on down faster, keeping an eye on
it, and then we saw you."

"I was tied to the raft out in the middle of the Rumpus,
and I was hollering my head off," I said.

"Littabelle," said Aunt Sorrow, "you want to tell this
story or you going to let me?"

"You can tell it," I said. "It's interesting. Every time
you tell it, it is."

"Your folks was gone," continued Aunt Sorrow. "We
didn't find their bodies till the next day. You know the
way the Rumpus seems to rise higher in the center during
a flood? It's caused by the drag of the water on the rocks
when it comes roaring around Vulture Bluff, Paw Paw
says. I never saw it so high as I saw it that day. You was
smack in it on your raft and it was pitchin' and spinnin',
and all around it there was logs bobbing and whole trees.
Even a possum on a log. A terrible flood. We thought
you'd be carried downriver in it, the way it tore past us
so fast, but then the raft you was on was hit by somethin'
underneath and nudged over to the bank on this side,
and Paw Paw shed his pants and shoes and jumped in

and rescued you. Hutchens should have been the one to do it. He was standin' right there, but he was a shirker then just like he is now."

Aunt Sorrow's word for Hutchens was a true one. He did not inherit his ancestors' pride in family or loyalty to it. Estie and Ora are the same way. They used to come whenever it suited them, and it was painful to see their behavior. Itching to get away hardly before greetings had been said, they'd sit on the porch with the old ones, talking about their city lives while Aunt Sorrow and I rushed to put dinner on the table. Then Aunt Sorrow would have me call dinner, and they'd come inside and eat our food and take more of it away with them. Chickens, butter, eggs, pounds of fresh-ground sausage if it was the season for it, and baskets of garden sass. Carrots, peas, lettuce, sweet corn and tomatoes. Occasionally one would suffer a twinge and offer to pay for what he took but in *such* a way. . . . Like a selfish child offering a lick of his ice cream cone. Not ever a dollar was accepted. In those days and still, Paw Paw and Maw Maw would give their skin for their children and gladly. The other way around was a different story except for Aunt Sorrow. She it was who provided the life comforts the old ones could not buy for themselves. Her money was hard come by. It was not a picnic to ride horseback around on the back roads and trails of these hills, ministering to the sick. I used to be a beekeeper and would add the profits from my crops to what she earned.

We are mountaineers, and people should envy our lives because they are better than any lived in towns, I am sure.

I have seen the towns, the main streets of them a-throng with loafers on Saturday afternoons. And tasted their water. And observed their restive children who mill around in the stores yammering for attention. It seems to me that town dwellers live faster and so miss too much of what is good. I think their children have never been entertained with winter-night tales of ghosts that haunt old deserted farmhouses. These stories are best when the snow is on the ground and the spirits of the dead are abroad. With luck and imagination you can look and see them perched in the bald, December branches.

In our hills, still, the leaf-bordered waterways flow pure and clean. Come October, when our trees are in color, they glow like lantern candles on the slopes of our hollows. Our stony acres receive the seeds of corn, sorghum and garden truck, and the song of the cardinal brings health and happiness to every home. The seasons run almost true to the calendar. Summers are the longest with the heat lying thick in the hollows, and there are quick, sometimes dangerous thunderstorms.

One afternoon, late in that summer I write about now, we were struck by lightning during one of these storms. It came just after the highest heat of the day had passed. Ahead of a big show of lightning flickering weirdly blue, green and yellow over the hills, the sky darkened and a chilly wind moved down from the timbered hillside. A great thunderhead formed directly above us and dust devils spouted in the dry valley road, spinning away clockwise. The clouds swelled with the coming rain.

Aunt Sorrow was puttering in a corner of the lower

half of our barn, which she used as a laboratory. She called to me, and we ran to take the clothes from the wash line, and Maw Maw called from the back doorway to Paw Paw to either come to the house or stay safe in the barn until the storm was over. Thunder began to pound the mountains. The trees on the slopes of them were being bent forward, some of them bowed almost to the snapping point, with the force of the pushing wind.

Aunt Sorrow and I were yanking the clothes from the line, letting the pins fall to the ground as they would. We finished, and I bent to lift the basket. The sky was gray-black and tumbling, and the lightning raced through the clouds. Aunt Sorrow was running to the house and yelling for me to follow. I hefted the basket and took two steps. I saw the lightning tear the clouds apart, and the wind lifted my beehives and carried them away into the gale. I remember clear my thought: all my work, saving them from the cold and starvation last winter, it was for nothing.

I saw the lightning, a flaming sword of it, run along the ground and zigzag in the space between the barn and the house, plowing the earth as a harrow does. It hit a tree in its path and a sheath of bark was blasted from its trunk in one piece. The lightning hit the house, heating the electrical wiring burning hot, and almost at once fire shot from the walls and roof. Nearly everything we owned and cherished was destroyed.

CHAPTER TWO

In these mountains our weathers will attack you one minute and smile on you the next. That day, after the fire had done its most and the storm had moved away from us toward the east, the sun shone again and some titlarks came from the grasses, swaggering their white-edged tails and giving their songs.

Paw Paw and Maw Maw stood together in front of our old Dutch-style barn and Paw Paw, over and over again, said, "Maw Maw, it could've been worse. Look on it this way. We could've all been killed."

"I'll never again set any store by lightning rods," said

Maw Maw, stunned. "Everything we had gone up in smoke. How can anything be that quick? It didn't even spare us any extra clothes. What'll we do?"

"For right now we will go to the Petifers," said Aunt Sorrow, referring to our neighbors and friends. "They'll take us in temporary."

The Petifers had sat out the storm in their potato house, which is a little one apart from their bigger one and actually a buried cyclone cellar. All of life is Ada Petifer's province. She makes handsome quilts and has a tribe of goats. Loves to set up with the sick. The only book she has ever read is the Word of God and she believes every letter in it. Her husband, Holtie, has a disposition to get his crops laid by early and then sit on his porch with his hat pulled low. Occasionally a wandering hunter or fisherman will roam into this hollow, which is known as Blue Ash. If, to Holtie, these waywards appear to be from the outside, he will skip out to meet them. One time he snagged a man from Boston, and I am sure this person was disappointed to describe the encounter to friends back home. For Holtie does not have an idiot countenance or a lipful of snuff. He keeps himself clean and most of the time wears shoes. He does not use tobacco. He is graceful—lean and fair with a fine, clear brow and steady, gray eyes. He has large, good intentions, which are seldom carried out, and believes in his superstitions. When he hears a mourning dove in the spring, he believes he will travel off in the direction the sound came from even if it is against his will. And he has a mesh wire stretched across the roof of his house to keep the whippoorwills away. If one should call from his housetop, there will be a death in his house.

In cash assets the Petifers are the same as we, hard-put to produce two dollars to rub together and usually in debt to the trading store at Pioneer Gap. General Birdwell used to be the proprietor of this store. General is his first name and not a military title. On muleback, General's brother Bobo carries the mail in and out of these mountains.

I do not like to give the feeling that we ever thought of ourselves as being totally poor. There is a side to our natures that allows us times of thinking we might be rich. When our corn is up and high enough for the ears to have formed, that is one. It is like looking at a rich, green parade. The leaves flow with the stream of the wind and the tops of the plants gleam like gold in the sun.

Holtie and Ada Petifer are not young. They believe, as some mountain people believe, that their futures are all laid out for them by non-human causes. What is to be will be. I will tell you I do not subscribe to this kind of thinking; it is mental indolence that serves as an excuse for the trouble of doing.

Holtie is afraid of God. The afternoon we got burned out he said he thought God had finally got him, the way the lightning cracked and sizzled all around his cyclone cellar. At one point during the fireworks, he was knocked to his knees. Ada said it wasn't the lightning that did it; said the thunder shook one of the ceiling beams loose and one end of it fell, conking Holtie on the head.

We spent that night with the Petifers. In this crisis at

first Paw Paw and Maw Maw were like little children, allowing Aunt Sorrow and Ada to tell them when to wash for supper, where to sit, and to take helpings of everything. After the meal Aunt Sorrow asked Ada for paper and pencil and instructed me to sit down and write letters to Hutchens, Estie and Ora, telling them what had happened.

"Do you think they will come?" asked Ada.

"No," replied Aunt Sorrow.

"It'd be a distance for them," said Paw Paw.

I said, "I think I should tell them if they cannot come they should send money."

"No," said Maw Maw. "Just tell them what's happened. They'll do what's right."

Holtie dared to say, "I do not think so. I do not think they will either send money or come. None of your kids, except Sorrow, has ever put themselves out any for you."

"Because Sorrow's never married and has always made her home with us," said Paw Paw, huffy and testy. "My other kids are just as good. Soon as they get Littabelle's letters, they'll come. I've been sittin' here a-thinkin'. You ever taken a good look at the inside of my barn, Holtie?"

"A couple of times," said Holtie.

"I've been sittin' here a-thinking we'll live in it till we can get a new house raised," said Paw Paw.

"You can't," said Holtie, aghast at the idea.

"Why not?" said Paw Paw. "It's ours. There's no law against it, I know about. It's clean. It don't leak. The animals wouldn't mind movin' over a little. We could live in the loft."

Holtie began to argue several objections. "There's no running water in it, is there?"

"No, but we got the creek just out the back door. We can carry our water from it till we can get a new house raised."

"Well," said Holtie, scratching for a straw. "At least you still got a nice outhouse. The lightning didn't get that. What'll you sleep on? And what'll you use for furniture?"

"We'll sleep in the hay, and I know how to make furniture," said Paw Paw. Sharp as a ferret after a prairie dog, he said, "Holtie, I'm goin' to raise a log cabin. I'll put it on the foundation where the old house was."

Holtie could not reject the thin note of entreaty in my grandfather's voice. There was something moral involved here. "I will help you," he said, making one of his scapegrace promises.

I should tell you about my uncle Hutchens and my aunts Ora and Estie. Hutchens thinks he is the captain of the town. He is not the captain of anything. He has chronic nasal catarrh and a wife named Mispah who is vain of her feet and legs. He is in business with Mispah's father, who is a land speculator, a hook-nosed Dutchman from Pennsylvania. Ora is married to a furniture-store owner named Clell who always has his mouth full of soda-mint tablets, and they have three children. Estie is married to a man named Tilman Spanhank. They operate a rooming house and have a daughter named Florine. Florine is two years my junior and wants to go to New York and be an actress. I do not know anything about that kind of life. An account like this is not so easy to write as you might imagine. I have to keep its events in their proper order, else it will not make sense.

We went back home the next day, Holtie and Ada with us. Maw Maw and Ada did the farm chores, and Holtie and Paw Paw went to the woods to look for stands of trees that would be suitable for house and furniture building. Aunt Sorrow and I spent the morning pulling things we thought might be of any use from the wreckage of the burned house, carrying them to the barn and up the ladder to the loft. All the while, doing this, Aunt Sorrow was saying there should be a law against children turning their backs on the needs of their parents. I said, "But they have not turned their backs yet. Not this time anyway. Bobo has not been by to pick up the letters to them yet."

"This time will not differ from any other time," said Aunt Sorrow. "Remember the time Maw Maw had the pleurisy and nearly died? They claimed they never got my letters, but I know they did. I know a lie when I see one."

I said, "When we get settled down again, I am going to go out and see can I find some stray bee swarms, and this time I am going to make my hive stands from something the wind cannot blow away."

"You are a good child," said Aunt Sorrow, "and I wisht you was my daughter instead of my niece." We built an outdoor cooking place in the yard, and for our noon dinner Maw Maw stewed a rooster. It was her idea to make use of the creek to keep our dairy foods from spoiling. Bright and cold, the creek straggles through this deep, winding hollow and is shallow except in the spring when the melting snows feed it or there is a cloudburst. Its water is made to appear green by the green understory and trees that crowd its shores. We women shed our shoes, hiked our skirts and waded out into the creek, scouting for flat stones; and with these constructed in a little cove of the stream an arrangement of watered ledges that would support pails of milk, bowls of butter and pans of eggs. We had a spring house.

There is a thing about the Lees which I should have told before now and it is this: Generally our ideas do not blow over easy. With or without Holtie's help, Paw Paw had it in his mind to put up a log cabin where the old house had stood and could not anybody detract him from doing it.

Holtie said, "Mr. Lee, sir, you will kill yourself doing it. Failing that, it won't be right when we get it up. *If* we do."

"Out in the woods this morning," said Paw Paw, "you said you knew all about raising a log cabin."

Holtie spent a moment with his conscience. "To tell you the truth," he admitted, "now that I have examined my memory I have to say I don't know anything about such an operation except you notch the logs to seat them."

"We can do that," said Paw Paw.

"And then you fill up the cracks with clay."

"That won't be hard," said Paw Paw.

"A man your age," said Holtie, "has got no business

out in the woods swingin' a axe. What if one of them trees was to fall on you?"

"I can get out of the way of any fallin' tree fast as you can," rejoined Paw Paw. He was itching to get back to the woods with his axe. After the trees were felled, they would be brought out of the woods by means of drag chains and mule-power. It was Paw Paw's plan to use the old, unmortared house foundation and to have the cabin erected and made liveable by the week of Thanksgiving.

By this time Holtie was feeling dreary about the whole thing. He remembered some urgent business of his own, and he and Ada went home but returned just before sundown with four quilts, a box of assorted clothing-garments, some food staples, two kerosene lanterns and some matches. From the debris of the burned-down house, Aunt Sorrow and I had salvaged a metal trunk containing sheets and crash towels. They were scorched but not ruined. Ada had remembered to supply us with some soap, and as soon as it was dark, Aunt Sorrow and I had a jaybird bath in the creek.

That night I slept in Ada's wedding dress. It was yellow and had a neck-to-hem ruffle. None of us was in any mood to hear a fool mockingbird show off his talents. From somewhere in back of the barn he sang his head off. Our hay-beds, spread with the scorched sheets and Ada's quilts, were not uncomfortable. The cows in the stalls beneath us kept us awake some with their twitchings and thumpings. From now on I will refer to my aunt merely as Sorrow.

CHAPTER THREE

Our stock of winter-standby foods had been destroyed in the fire. Sorrow's sun-dried fruits; Maw Maw's home-canned fish, poultry and vegetables; bushels of potatoes, parsnips, onions and cabbages. The cellar beneath our old kitchen had to be cleaned of the ruined foodstuffs. Sorrow and I took shovels to it the second day. It was a mess and heartsickening.

There was a man at Pintail Fork owing Sorrow a substantial sum in patient's fees, and on the third day following our calamity, just after noon had passed, I saddled my burro, Little Boy, and Sorrow her horse, Hookey, and we set out to go there. Our trail had to be one of our own decision since, on this side of the Rumpus River, there was, at that time, only the road going from Pioneer Gap to Blue Ash Hollow and no farther. The river was to our right, and we rode through some of the wildest and roughest land in the Ozarks. We had glimpses of white-tailed deer, opossums and fox squirrels. We saw a band of blue-winged teal in low flight. Along the river's shoreline, flowers were in bloom, great stretches of red lobelia and purple bergamot. We turned away from the river and started an upward climb through a zone of rocky hills. Pintail Fork lay on the other side of these.

Hookey, who did not get his name without a reason, was showing some spirit, wanting to investigate every sound and motion. Sorrow indulged him as she always did and gave him rein. He lifted his head and broke into an easy trot and then a run and in just a minute was far ahead of Little Boy and me. He carried Sorrow up a rise and disappeared into the line of summit trees there. This happened very fast.

There was no need for alarm. I thought there was not, for Sorrow was a good horsewoman and Hookey was sure of foot. Little Boy and I took our time ascending the rise. The sunshine was strong and we were commanded to a fine view.

Oh, but on the other side of that summit there was a ravine, cut there by the flow of water, issuing from an underground cavern. It contained fast-running, waist-high water and murderous-looking rocks. There was no warning of this; if you did not pull up tight and fast at the edge of the summit, you stood more than a fair chance of tumbling down the cliff and into it. Sorrow and Hookey had done just that, and there had been no sound to it that I had heard.

I have always thought burros had more sense than horses. Little Boy pulled up short on the edge of the cliff above the ravine, and I looked down and saw the slovenly path Sorrow and Hookey had taken in falling to the gully below. A carbine borrowed from Holtie Petifer, a sun hat inherited from Ada Petifer just that morning, Sorrow's eyeglasses and a tin drinking cup were strewn. The grass was mauled, and there were dislodged rocks. Hookey himself must have taken a terrible mauling going down. There was blood on his face-blaze, his rump hide was torn. He was floundering in the eddying water, trying to stand, but he kept falling. Sorrow had either been thrown to the opposite of the gully or had crawled there. She was sitting on its bank with her feet in the water.

Ordering Little Boy to stay where he was, I dismounted and scrambled down. Sorrow raised her head to watch me but did not speak. When I was within conversation distance, I said, "Are you hurt?"

"No. Try to help Hookey. He will drown if you don't get him out of there." It was as if she were giving me an order to perform something commonplace. I waded out to Hookey but couldn't get close enough to him to take hold of his reins. His eyes were berserked. He did not know me and he kept rising and falling. I could hear his struggle for breath.

Sorrow looked so queer. She was not unduly excited. "Littabelle?"

"I don't know if I can get him out of here, Aunt Sorrow. I think he's hurt bad. He is breathing funny, and I think one of his legs is broken."

Sorrow pulled her feet from the water and stood but had to sit again quickly, a hand to her forehead. There was red froth on Hookey's mouth. I wondered how long he could continue his agitated efforts. I was not calm. The thought came to me that even if I could manage to get close enough to him to grab his reins, he might bite or kick me and that I was going to have to make a lone decision. It was quite a thing to be out there in the numbing water with the pain-crazed horse. Every time he would fall I would be drenched anew and his strangled snortings were terrible to hear. Sorrow had her chin on her knees. She was silently watching.

I left off trying to do anything for Hookey and waded in to Sorrow. She looked up at me. "I am not hurt," she said. "Only dizzy from the fall. Please go back and help Hookey."

I said, "Aunt Sorrow, I don't know what to do for him. He is bleeding at the mouth, and I am sure one of his legs is broken. Maybe more than one. He doesn't know me and will not let me near him. What should I do?"

"I cannot think. My head is buzzing. Why are you crying? That never did any good."

"I do not know," I said. "I do not know what to do for Hookey. He is my friend as much as yours. I have always loved him."

"Yes," said Sorrow, calm as ice. "You and I have always loved Hookey and Little Boy and Maw Maw and Paw Paw and each other. We are not like Hutchens or

Estie or Ora, thank our good Lord."

I had to make the judgment to destroy Hookey alone, for Sorrow, it was plain to see, was in a condition of shock and was in no way able to aid. I left her and waded back through the gully to the other side of it and went up the side of the down-drop to where the carbine and the other things were strewn. Above me on the grassy plateau, Little Boy was peacefully grazing, and I envied him. Animals survive better the loss of friends than humans, I think. They merely watch. The poor human suffers. He shakes and shudders and his own living, for a minute, is death to him.

I put a bullet in Hookey that afternoon, and he settled in the water. After that Sorrow, Little Boy and I went on to Pintail Fork. Sorrow's patient there was Merlie Bud Luckabill. His town was made up of houses in a group on a hillside, a school building, a square, white-stone church and a filling-station–cafe-store. Children in the schoolyard were playing pom-pom-pullaway. They stopped their game long enough to watch us pass. Children are not graceful in all their gestures. One of those watching us pass his playground left his comrades and ran out into our path to show us his long, red tongue. "Bwaaaaaa," he said. Had the circumstances been more on my side, I might have taken the time to teach him a manner or two.

Merlie Bud Luckabill was a little gamecock of a man with a wife three times his size. Her given name was Dovie, and her hair was so red it shone like a bonnet of fire in the sun. Anything in her path stood in peril of being knocked aside or trampled. "What's the matter with the Doc?" she bawled, rushing from her porch to greet us. "She's not snakebit, is she? Merlie Bud will help her down; don't you try to do it, Littabelle. Oh, she gets white, don't she? Hold on, Doc. Don't pass out on us. Merlie Bud, you'll have to pick her up and carry her. She has passed out."

To me, Merlie Bud's ability to carry anything besides himself looked doubtful. He wore a pair of knee-length pants and beneath the hems of these his legs appeared ill, the blood vessels in them contorted and enlarged, purplish in color. Later on in the day I asked him what his condition was, and he said varicose veins. For years Sorrow had doctored him for this ailment.

The Luckabills did not excite easily. With cold water and a little tipple of some white-lightning whiskey they brought Sorrow around and then took her to a quiet part of their house to rest in one of their feather beds. Merlie Bud offered the opinion that she might have suffered a skull concussion. After a cup of tea with the Luckabills, I went to look in on her. She was not delirious; I cannot say that. She said some queer things to me though:

"Don't be afraid, Littabelle, honey."

I told her a fat lie. "I am not afraid, Aunt Sorrow. You are going to be all right."

"If I should die here, don't waste any time squallin' over me. Let Merlie Bud and Dovie arrange things. They are good friends and will know how to wangle it. Don't let them lay out any cash on me. They don't have any to spare. Just put me in a hole and cover me up."

"Aunt Sorrow," I said, "I am not going to put you in any hole. Nobody is."

"Don't let anybody set up with me after I'm gone. If you can't get a preacher for me, let Merlie Bud say what he will over me. When he ain't sick, he's the school teacher here so he'll know what to say. Don't let anybody shroud the mirrors, afraid my spirit will be lookin' in the glass. It won't be. Just put me in the ground and go on back to Maw Maw and Paw Paw. Don't let them grieve too much."

I felt severely divided from her, and it was a bad moment. People are detestably selfish. From cradle to grave they think persons they love have nothing to do but please them. Their perpetual cry is, "Don't leave me." That is what I wanted to say to Sorrow then: *Don't leave me.* I could not. The words would not come.

"This is a nice bed," said Sorrow. "Nicer'n any we've ever had. Nicer'n any we've got now, for sure. If you have to bury me here, don't let Hutchens or Ora or Estie know where I am. Tell 'em you forgot where you put me. I don't want any of 'em snivelin' over me. They're shite-pokes, all three of them. If I could have my way, none of 'em would ever set eyes on Maw Maw or Paw Paw again. I'd have them put in jail for their neglect. Somebody should make a law for such. I would, had I the education."

I watched her and kept quiet, thinking she would drop off to sleep. In a minute she commenced to talk of past things. "Littabelle, you remember that time you found out there wasn't no Santa Claus?"

I said I did not, and she said, "You was six mebbe. We always had rice for breakfast because it was cheap, and you said you was tired of it. I told you you'd have to eat it 'cause it was all we had and said you'd have to sit at the table till your dish of it was gone."

"Did I eat it?"

"No. Maw Maw and Paw Paw went to the fields and I went to make the beds. You sat where you was, lookin' at that dish of rice. When I got back to the kitchen half an hour later, it was gone. You had pitched it out the door. I looked out and saw it layin' on the ground, but you said you didn't do it. I said I'd whip you for tellin' me a lie. You said it wasn't a lie, and I whipped you. I said I had never lied to you and I didn't want you to ever lie to me."

"Your color is coming back," I said. "You must be feeling stronger. Could you sleep some now?"

"You didn't squall," said Sorrow. "I raised you not to ever do much of that. But a couple of hours later you came tearin' in just a-bawlin' to me about Santa Claus. You said I had told you a lie about there being one and ought to be whipped myself for doing it. Said you had known for a year there wasn't no such person but had just remembered it. Littabelle, you were right. I should have been whipped myself for telling you there was a Santa Claus. There sure isn't. The world is a bad place, Littabelle. I should have told you that a long time ago. The world is a bad place and most people in it are bad. They will lie to you and thieve from you. If you be weak enough to let them, they'll pack all their responsibilities off on to you and they'll run away to have the good times, and you can work at what they've left till you drop in your tracks and still you'll not have done much."

I said, "Aunt Sorrow." And she turned her head and her faint smile asked my forgiveness for her little outburst. She always did that after a moment of harshness, this little dove of a woman, sweet of eye and smile. Her second given name is Patience; it should have been Charity, the kind that is love and goodness in action. So many people suffered less because of this fair, giving person.

"Aunt Sorrow," I said.

And with a queer kind of wilted regret she gazed at me. "Littabelle," she said, "if you have to bury me here, be sure to tell The Hermit where I am and be his friend. He is a fine man." She was referring to a man who lived at Vulture Bluff—a strong, eastern Yankee who, at one time, had been sappy-in-love with her. She never said so, but I always thought she and The Hermit had a falling-out over her family loyalty. I can remember the year he stopped coming around so often. It was not right, but Sorrow never let on to any hurt. She was a lover of the kind of romance seen in bobolink meadows in spring when all the world comes to a surge. We used to go out and gather the plants for her herb-medicines during that season.

She always had to skip ahead of me on those trips. With our baskets containing our cutting and digging tools slung over our arms, we would start out together, but she was never the kind to merely walk along a path watching her shoes. She would sight the gleam of a leaf or a spot of color and would bound off wayward, calling me to follow. She was never without her magnifying glass, and I would be required to squat until my legs numbed, having the ways of the woodland plants explained to me. "Look, Littabelle, it's a jack-in-the-pulpit. See the way it blooms even before it gets its leaves? See its little green-and-purple coat? This is a young plant and now it's a male but in four or five years, after it's stored up enough food, it'll become a female. Isn't that interesting?"

"Yes," I would say. "Is he of any use?"

"Sure. Everything's of some use. You can take the roots of this little fella and partly dry them, and for a person who needs to sweat, that'll turn the trick in a hurry. This plant is good to help a cold, too. No, don't try to taste it; it'll scald your mouth. It's poison unless it's dried and doctored right."

So many of Sorrow's plants had their oddities. She was like them. Bountiful but managed wisely, they give a confidence in God.

The Luckabills persuaded Sorrow and me that it would be best if we stayed the night with them, although I said this might give Paw Paw and Maw Maw something to worry about. Dovie said, "Shoot, it won't either. They'll know you've stayed over when you don't show up come dark."

By suppertime Sorrow said she was fully recovered from her fall except for little seizures of dizziness and the headache. She looked sick to me, and I kept thinking of the way Hookey had met his death. Merlie Bud paid Sorrow all of the money he owed her. She ate a little and went back to her bed.

Probably of all the people in this big windy of mine, the Luckabills were the most swayful. They had a grand-boy by the name of L. C. who put in his appearance as Merlie Bud, Dovie and I were finishing our evening meal. I thought we might be of around the same age and that I could see through him as you can see through most males. Generally they are in a rush to tell you all of their affairs in five minutes and want to impress on you their superior energies and sense.

I could not see through L. C. Luckabill any more than you can see through a bat of brick. He had a splendid bush of red-gold hair and his sleepy eyes revealed no innermost workings. He wanted to know if I liked children, and for some fool reason I said, "I am not married and never intend to be."

He said, "I think they are the most interestin' people on the face of the earth. Just think what the world'd be like if there wasn't any here."

I said, "I never thought they were God's messengers."

"What's that mean?"

"Nothing. I was a child once. When I think back on the years I was one, I have to shudder. That little kid, making all those mistakes."

"Uh-huh," said L. C. "That's what I am talking about. Somebody has got to teach children not to make mistakes."

I said, "Well, I am laying off other plans for myself."

"Would you like to see the town?" asked L. C.

"I've seen it," I answered. "This is not my first visit here."

Dovie and Merlie Bud urged me to go out for a while

with L. C. Sorrow was asleep, and there wasn't anything else to do, so I went.

Pintail Fork was closed for the night. A fine, white mist was creeping down from the highlands, and from the autumn grasses and pumpkin patches of the hillside houses, whippoorwills chanted. We sat on the steps of the church for a while and I said, "What do you do?"

"I live here," said L. C.

"Besides that."

"I work."

"Doing what?"

"I raise things for my mother and me and other people."

"What things?"

"Oats. Turkeys. And I'm a guide for anybody wants to hire one."

"My grandfather gave me some turkeys once when I was little but they all drowned in the rain."

"And I teach school sometimes."

"You?"

"When my grandpa isn't feelin' good, like today. You ever thought about bein' a teacher?"

"No."

"You don't believe in women working for their living?"

"I believe in it. Women have to. God gave us the meanest load to carry. It'd kill the normal man to do all I do in one day. He'd have to go to bed for a week."

Some mist had settled on L. C.'s hair. His face seemed to spring at me. "The examination to be a substitute teacher here isn't hard. My grandpa gives it. Do you know how to parse a sentence?"

I said, "I suppose I do as well as the next one. The teacher at Pioneer Gap where I went to school was a man, so I didn't learn much. I was a terrible pupil though, so I cannot blame it all on him."

"Are you through with your schooling?"

"I was through with it a long time ago," I said. "But the law said I had to keep on putting in my time."

L. C. Luckabill's purpose in getting me to sit on the steps of the church house that hazy evening in Pintail Fork was to get me to say I would take the examination to be substitute teacher when Merlie Bud was unable to work. L. C. said I could ride Little Boy from home to Pintail Fork on teaching days. I began to see through him.

"That is a long, hard trip by burro," I said, funning with him a little. "I love Little Boy and would not dream of asking him to share such a thing with me."

L. C. made a reach, as we say; he delivered a little sermon on the joys of teaching children. I then told him I was not interested in any part of the proposition.

L. C. said, "Well, I guess I made a mistake. You are not as smart as I thought you might be."

"I am smart enough."

"It is a good offer," said L. C. "The pay is fair, and you would be doing something useful."

"I am useful enough as I am. You would think so if you could see me traipsing around these mountains with Aunt Sorrow, trying to get medical help to sick people when it is winter and there are two feet of snow on the ground."

"I have wasted a couple of hours on you," said L. C.

"I did not ask you to," I said. Then he lost his temper and said it was no wonder to him I was not married. As unreasonable and homely as I was, who would have me? He let me walk back to Merlie Bud's and Dovie's house alone.

As I passed one of the hillside houses, a little boy appeared out of the mist to greet me. "Hey, lady. Where you goin', lady?"

"That is none of your business," I said. "Get out of my way."

He stood in front of me, spraddle-legged and with his arms outspread. "I might have somethin' to tell you, lady."

"What?"

He said, "Me and L. C. was watchin' you through our spyglass this afternoon."

"Watching from where, little boy?"

The boy lifted an arm and made a sweep with it. "We was out there. Watchin' things. L. C. was mad today at Royce Fredericks because he ate a box of chalk and got sick, so we all got to go on a field trip to look at flowers and birds. You ride a burro real good, lady."

I said, "Royce Fredericks must be demented. Chalk is not anything to be put in your stomach."

"L. C. said you was going to be the new teacher to take Mr. Luckabill's place from now on when he's sick. I'm getting ready for you, lady."

"How's that?"

This child looked like a young ape. It was not so dark that I did not get a good look at him. He had a fuzzy, oversized head and a little flat nose and he grinned at me with his eyes askance. "I just said I was gettin' ready for you, lady, if you be the new teacher going to take Mr. Luckabill's place when he's sick."

This child's name was Salem Cayce, and it came to be my belief that he had some kind of nervous disorder for it was impossible for him to sit or stand still for over two minutes at a time. He was twelve. Eventually we got to be the best of friends, and one snowy afternoon he suggested to me that a witch might have spelled and fitified him. Whether this was a true trouble or not, I cannot say. If it was, it did not hinder his courage or intelligence any. One day Salem and I performed emergency surgery on Royce Fredericks and I have to say this: Even when the blood came from Royce's throat and Salem got some of it on his hands, he did not flinch.

I am getting ahead of my story and must make a bigger attempt to keep the events of it in their proper order.

CHAPTER FOUR

Sorrow and I went home the next day, she looking frangible but disavowing any leanings toward feeling ill. I did not want Little Boy to have to carry a double load and walked beside him and Sorrow. I suggested that we make frequent rest stops, and Sorrow did not have to be urged.

Dovie Luckabill had loaned a light "just-in-case" blanket and provided a basket of food. Avoiding the region where Hookey had met his death, we went down into and across deep-cut valleys and encountered only two trout anglers trying their luck in a headwater. They watched us pitch temporary camp beside the stream, and I thought they handled themselves inexpertly. Sorrow was disdainful of them. "Flatlanders," she said. "Even if they was stark naked, I could tell you that. The one in the red shirt has got rheumatism. Look at the way he stands to go after them fish. He's rump-sprung. Time he's my age he'll be in a wheel chair—if he gets that far."

The two flatlanders ogled us while trying to appear disinterested in our doings. Sorrow said she did not care what they thought of us. Beneath an elm tree I spread the blanket and she laid down on it and almost immediately was asleep. Presently the two fishermen departed, and while Little Boy poked and sniffed among the fern and wildflowers growing amass along the bank of the stream, I harvested enough watercress to provide us and the Petifers with salad greens for several days.

In her rest Sorrow looked more her age. It wasn't natural for her to want to sleep during the day. I sat beside her, watching her breathe. She woke and we ate our noon meal from Dovie's basket and I showed her the watercress I had gathered and she said, "Oh, Maw Maw will like that but it'll wilt 'fore we get home if you don't wet it and wrap it in something. Some moss would be the thing. In a minute we'll go look for some."

Why is it that always, just before a destruction, things seem to be at their pleasantest? We were in a region of the Ozarks that dripped and gushed and sang. The sun lay on the face of our stream, and the handsome autumn flower heads a-bloom all along its shoreline were startling to the eye. I, because I had always been instructed in that manner, and Sorrow, because it was her nature to give attention to the beauties of the world, had never wasted ourselves when in such locations. I had never known Sorrow to allow either of us to spendthrift time in the presence of what God and the ages had created. So that day it was a curiosity for her to ignore the rich life all around us and take up conversation concerning commoner subjects. From a knot in her handkerchief she took the money Merlie Bud Luckabill had paid her and, while examining the printing on each bill, began to talk in a most irregular way. "For a person to cut off his days the way I have for the sake of others is self-murder," she said. "It's a crime against the Lord's intentions."

It was a bad thing to hear. This sentiment must have been locked up in her for years and years. I knew she had reference to her years of doing for Maw Maw and Paw Paw and me and could not blame her for her feeling, yet what was there to say in reply?

"That shitepoke Hutchens," she said. "And Ora and Estie too. Their chickens are all going to come to roost some day. They've got theirs coming. I haven't been able to see to it, but someday somebody will. Where'd you get that dress, Littabelle?"

Surprised, because she had been the one to hand it to me from Ada Petifer's box, I said, "Why, it was in the box Ada Petifer gave us."

"Looks like something Misery might have donated," she said. "You ever noticed the way Misery walks, Littabelle?"

"She's got pretty legs," I said.

Sorrow said, "She walks like she's been followin' a plow all her life. When we get home, I want you to burn that dress. Yellow is no color for a young girl. And either put your hair up or cut it off. You look like a Indian squaw with it a-hangin' down your back like that."

I recalled the only Indian woman I had ever seen. She was dead, stark-naked and lost, in the back of a flatbed wagon pulled up in front of General Birdwell's store. Two woodsmen had found her in the hills above General's store and had brought her in. Every man, woman and child in Pioneer Gap came to rubber and gawk at her. The two rescuers could not be persuaded to take her away. "Take her away where?" they asked. "She don't belong to us. We never seen her before. We just found her in the woods. We thought she might belong to one of you-uns."

General was a burly man, but he had a disposition to grow faint and sick when in the presence of anything just the least bit off-color. He ran back into his store, snatched the first covering he could lay his hands on, and ran back out with it. As he covered the grinning, dead Indian woman with several yards of lovely blue dress material, her two rescuers disengaged their horses from the wagon and took them to the livery stable. There must have been a law to cover the situation but if there was, nobody in Pioneer Gap knew anything about it. The woman stayed in the wagon in front of General's store overnight, and then he was obliged to have her buried at his own expense.

Sorrow did not remember the incident. She still clutched her money in one hand and with the other was smoothing her hair and eyebrows. "You remember the durndest things."

I said, "Even if that woman was dead, I thought she had pretty hair."

Sorrow said, "Let's go to Little Rock."

I said, "What?"

"You've never been. It's time you went. Let's go now, why don't we? Why don't you and me and Little Boy not go home just yet? Why not we just keep on going down the mountains till we get to Little Rock?"

"I doubt the governor would be overjoyed to see us come riding into his town on the back of Little Boy," I said.

Said Sorrow, "I know the governor personally. He'd be glad enough to see me again. He oughta be. I saved his life one time."

"When was that?" I asked, thinking we were merely engaging in a little foolery.

"You remember. That time he came to our house? It was, let me see, last spring. And I diagnosed him as havin' the dropsy and sent you out to look for some elderberries to make medicine for him."

"I went out last spring looking for elderberries to make medicine for the governor of the state of Arkansas? Because he had the dropsy? Aunt Sorrow, I couldn't have. Elders don't age their berries until September or October."

"We boiled them down with some honey," said Sorrow, obstinate and queer in her mistake.

I was not alarmed. Little Boy had climbed a nearby slope and was wandering around through the hickories and sour gums there. I stood up to watch him. I whistled to him and he turned in our direction, head lifted. I missed seeing Sorrow take up Holtie Petifer's carbine, which was lying on the blanket alongside of her. She emptied it into the air. The explosions from it sounded and resounded throughout the long, narrow valley. She did this in calm and spoke in calm. "That is what I am going to do to those three shitepokes, Hutchens, Ora and Estie. When they get around to comin', I am going to stand them in the road and make them dance. Is there any more ammunition for this gun?"

I said there was not. I was alarmed, for Sorrow did not look herself. She spat on the ground, the way low, country women do. The Lee women do not spit and neither do the Lee men. There is nothing more silent than the silent forest. I do not remember thinking of any hazard to myself, but I must have because I do remember being relieved there was no more ammunition for the gun. Sorrow was looking at me with her eyes a-glint.

When you begin, for any reason, to fear for someone you love, then you begin to fear for yourself. That is the way of it. You think—something has happened to this loved one. What is it? Why isn't there something to show? You try to think—what caused it?

The only cause I could think of was Sorrow's fall. When there is an insult to the head such as the one Sorrow had suffered in her fall from the cliff, the worst in us becomes master, I think. That is what I started to think that day, and it was not a bad imagining. You will see that it was not.

I reasoned Sorrow out of the notion of going to Little

Rock. She complained of headache and gave in. It was almost as if she had never thought of it in the first place. I whistled for Little Boy to come, we broke camp and continued our journey homeward, passing through a rainglen where we tarried long enough to gather moss for the already wilted watercress.

As we were nearing home, Sorrow said to me, "I don't want Maw Maw and Paw Paw to know about my accident, Littabelle."

"They will ask about Hookey," I said.

"We will tell them we met up with a band of wild mustangs and Hookey ran off with them."

"That will not sound reasonable. There have probably not been any wild horses in this neck of the woods for years. I have never seen one."

"Because you don't look as close at things as I do," she said. "There are all kinds of wild things out here. Why, just last week I saw a herd of buffalo." I was walking ahead of her a little and I did not want to turn to see her expression. She was not joking. "I want a Lee promise from you to not say anything about my accident to nobody. Not ever."

I tried to squirm out of giving it. A Lee promise is more sacred than a swear on the Bible. "Oh, look at the little cliff swallows," I said.

"A Lee promise," she said, and I had to give it. The untruth about Hookey and the wild mustangs was not important. Maw Maw and Paw Paw believed it, and it spared them the grief they would have had otherwise. It was the look in Sorrow's eyes that was important. This was a disturbance of things hard to title; the look was so brilliant and it spoke a secret, cunning language. It would come two or three times a day, and whenever I would see it start, I would turn away. I kept saying to myself—you are wrong about this. She is the same.

I was not wrong. She was not the same. I said to her, "Since I got through with school last June and am not ever going back to it, why don't I figure out a way to make some money? We could sure use some."

"You are spoiled-rotten," she said. "And a little on the lazy side too. I think you had better be lookin' around for somebody to marry."

"I am never going to marry," I said. "I am never going to leave you and Paw Paw and Maw Maw. Maybe next time we go for supplies, I will ask General Birdwell if he does not need some help in his store."

"We are all going to die here in this barn this winter," said Sorrow. "I know it, and so I am not making any plans for another thing. Except one." She got the indefinite loan of Holtie Petifer's carbine and bought a supply of ammunition from him and then had me write a postcard to Hutchens, ordering him to come at once and bring Estie and Ora with him. Hutchens, by return mail, replied that he, Estie and Ora would come as soon as they could. I looked for a big ruckus.

By the aft part of the week, Holtie and Paw Paw, with some of my help and Sorrow's, had completed one room of our new log house, mannered somewhat in the construction style of the pioneers. The minute the day pinked in, we were at it and we did not allow ourselves to quit until the sun had gone down. Holtie said the walls were "antigodlin" and to demonstrate what he meant, held a plumb bob to each one of them. Sure enough, the walls leaned slightly inward. Paw Paw was only momentarily put out. "Well," he said, "they aren't perfect, but who's going to be a-knowing that, except us to ourselves?"

Holtie was disapppinted. He went home for his noon dinner and did not come back. Paw Paw sent me to find out the reason. Holtie was piled up in the swing on his front porch with two pillows to his back. He looked whipped, and I said to him if his back was sore, he should have Sorrow prescribe for him.

He sat up and looked at me, disconsolate. "It's not only my back that's hurtin' me."

"Two or three applications of leopard's-bane to ailing muscles and they are as good as new," I said. "It is a vulnerary of tremendous power."

"I am not studying my muscles or my back or any vulnerary," said Holtie. "I am sittin' here thinking about you people. How you think you're going to make out this comin' winter? Has any of you stopped to think?"

"There are a few growing things left in our fields," I said. "And we are going to butcher soon as the first cold snap comes. And if we cannot squeak by on what we have then, why, General Birdwell will trust us for what we need."

"There ain't enough left in your fields to set two Sunday dinners," said Holtie. "I looked. You stripped your fields clean the first time around. And you can't live just on pork and dairy all winter. And I'll tell you somethin' else: General Birdwell isn't going to be so free with his credit as he's been in the past. He told me that. He's carryin' so much on his books now he's almost bankrupt hisself."

I said, "I am thinking about getting me a job. I would go to the city to do it, but I cannot leave Maw Maw and Paw Paw and Sorrow. I think I will ask General if he can give me some work in his store."

"It hurts me and Ada to see you people havin' to do the way you do," said Holtie. "Your grandpa ought to sell out and move."

"Our land is not worth anything except to us," I said. "To get the value from it, we have to live on it."

Holtie's glowering look acknowledged this truth. He took off on another tack. "Hutchens and Ora and Estie should be up here helpin' your grandpa put up the new house. 'Course I know that just ain't goin' to happen. They should at least send some money. Have they?"

"No."

"They ain't worth shootin', Littabelle."

"They are my blood relatives," I said, not in defense of them but because I had my pride.

"If they was any relationship to me, I'd find a way to force them to do what was right. Gripey-assed whiners."

Ada, who had come out on the porch, said, "Holtie."

"Well that's what they are," said Holtie. "I can't help it if it don't sound nice. It gripes me whenever they do break down and come. You ever heard 'em be anything but gripey-assed and whiney? You're a liar if you say so. All three ought to be strung up by their heels from the nearest Judas tree."

Ada said, "Littabelle, don't pay any attention to Holtie."

"She better had," said Holtie. "Winter's comin' and it's going to be a hard one. And we aren't a-gonna be here to help none."

"We have to go to Louisiana tomorrow," explained Ada. "Holtie's brother is bad-off sick. Bobo Birdwell just brought us the word a few minutes ago."

I said, "We will watch your place while you are gone, Holtie."

"No," said Holtie. " 'Twon't be necessary. Ada's cousin is comin' tomorrow, and we'll get her to look after the animals and stuff while we're away. She's not sociable, but we'll worry less, knowin' she's here. I'll bring my chair-makin' tools up to your granddaddy before we go. Don't let him use hickory that's too green, Littabelle. It should only be half-green. You drive a dry rung into a too-green post, it'll bust on you every time."

The tag-end warmth of the Ozark summer was still with us then, but the days of this were numbered. In the glimmering blue haze lying in the hollows and over the hills late in the afternoons I could see our true autumn. I thought I could smell the frosts of our Indian summer. Sorrow said I was rushing things. She was so testy nobody dared to say a word to her without trying it twice on himself.

Two days after the Petifers left to go to Louisiana, Hutchens, Ora and Estie came. Not all the way though. They were obliged to stop in the turn-around just beyond the line of our front fence and lean their heads out of the windows of Hutchens' car and speak to Sorrow that way, for she was holding Holtie Petifer's carbine on them. She threatened to shoot all three of them. Hutchens called out, "For cryin' out loud, Sorry, what's the matter with you? It's us! Ora, Estie and I!"

Sorrow did not have her eyeglasses on. She hardly ever wore them, for they were not necessary to her vision except when doing fine work. Feigning the inability to recognize her brother by his voice, she called back, "I can't recognize you by your voice, Hutchens! I broke my glasses yesterday! You got Misery with you?"

"Who?" shrieked Hutchens.

"Misery! Your wife! Is she with you? Tell her to stick her laig outa the window. Then I'll know it's you and not some trifler-wolf in sheep's clothing!"

Estie put her head all the way out of her window. "Sorrow, for the love of God!"

"Who is that female?" challenged Sorrow, squinting. Against her shoulder, Holtie's carbine was steady as a rock.

Ora's head came all the way out of her window. "Sorrow, have you gone crazy? Stop this foolishness! You can see us, plain as we can see you! Take that gun off us!"

"All of you get out of your car and stand in front of it," ordered Sorrow. Maw Maw and Paw Paw had come to the door of the barn loft. It was early morning, about seven o'clock. The sun was just beginning to pink and the vapor curling up from the creek was white and dense.

Paw Paw called out, "Sorrow! Sorrow! What're you doing?"

Sorrow ignored Paw Paw. She spoke again to the three

in the car. "All of you get out of your car and stand in front of it." I was standing in back of her about three feet removed, and she said, without turning her head, "Litta-belle, what's that noise?"

"It is me swallowing," I said. I thought I should try to take the carbine away from Sorrow, but I could not make my feet move me to her side. It is one thing to write about it now and another to have stood there, a viewer to this proceeding. I wondered why Hutchens did not crank up his car and leave. Sorrow might have put bullets in all of his tires had he tried.

Paw Paw and Maw Maw were both yelling from the doorway of the barn loft. Hutchens, Ora and Estie were coming out of Hutchens' car. They stood in front of it, and Sorrow emptied her carbine into the ground between their feet. She made them dance. When this was done she hurled her weapon against the fence, lifted her skirt, whirled and sped away. Across the footbridge that spanned the creek and into the woods.

In order to keep himself standing, Hutchens was having to supply himself with the support of the hood of his car. To my memory, Ora and Estie had never been overly fond of each other but in this situation they clung, their faces white as salt. "Oh. Oh," said Estie, dazed.

"She's gone crazy," said Hutchens. "I swear she has."

CHAPTER FIVE

Having shared and survived Sorrow's piece of devil-mischief, the three shitepokes from civilization drew themselves up proud and were aggrieved. There is nothing more unChristian in the human nature than the sufferings of the martyr who becomes one in order to be excused his own shortcomings. Hutchens made this pronouncement to Maw Maw and Paw Paw: "I do not know what has got into Sorrow, but whatever it is I assure you it better not show itself to me again."

"She has not been herself lately," said Maw Maw. "Sorrow would not hurt a flea. You know that."

"I don't know my sister any more," said Hutchens. "We are strangers. What's she mad at me about? I never did nothing to her."

Ora said, "We came up here, all three of us, to put in a day's work on the new house. Dragged ourselves out of bed at a terrible hour. I don't see how we can stay now. God only knows what next Sorrow will brood up in her mind for us."

"When she comes out of the woods," said Estie, "you can give her a message for me. Tell her it will be a cold day in July 'fore I come back. I know when I'm not welcome."

"Don't hold any hard feelings against your sister," said Maw Maw. "Don't. She's not been herself lately for some reason."

"Probably," said Ora, "she's going through the change of life. If that is her trouble, she would do well to prescribe for herself before she gets herself into a serious strait."

"Estie," said Ora, "you have the queerest ideas. Sorrow is not in no change of life. She is as sane as you or me. That was just a put-on for us. For what, who knows? I for one am not going to try and figure it out. I have enough personal troubles of my own without takin' on somebody else's."

Hutchens, who could sometimes show amazing flushes of feeling, said, "Awright, awright, it's finished. Maybe you got the time to stand around here talkin' about it but I haven't. Paw Paw, you and Holtie are doin' a good job on the new house. Looks good."

"Holtie says the walls are antigodlin," remarked Paw Paw. "You notice it, Hutchens?"

"Not a bit," declared Hutchens. "They look straight as ramrods to me. Are you-all comfortable in the barn, Paw Paw?"

"We're snug enough," replied Paw Paw. "Holtie and Ada have gone to Louisiana. His brother is bad-off sick."

Hutchens asked, "They won't be gone long, will they?"

"No," replied Paw Paw, as if he knew this to be a fact.

"I think we'd best not stick around here today," said Hutchens. "Not with the frame of mind Sorrow is in."

I did not think I was wrong in making this surmisal of Hutchens, Estie and Ora: However lick-penny their feelings of responsibility toward Maw Maw and Paw Paw had been, they were now, in their own minds, relieved of them. They could go back to town and tell their families and friends that their sister had run them off the family homestead with a carbine.

The three shitepokes got in Hutchens' car and left. I should think of a better word than shitepoke to use when I speak of them. It is too innocent to apply to Hutchens, Ora and Estie.

Paw Paw said he thought he, Maw Maw and I should just hang loose until our wits could be collected. He retrieved Holtie Petifer's gun from the bushes and built a little fire in the outdoor cooking place. We drank some tea. I was then sent to the woods to scout for Sorrow.

The weather of that day was somewhat askew. While the sun shone yellow-bright on the hills, a fresh wind raced around through the hollows. I could taste a coming rain. Seedtime was past, yet there was still colorful bloom. In this kind of weather, in this land, there is a sense of drifting. There is a green tint to the hills; there are rust-colored patches on the slopes. The heads of the stout, rigid teasels are dry to the touch.

I had an idea where Sorrow might have hied to; a secret place, thick with shrubby Judas trees. In this glade I had once been commissioned Captain of the Huckleberry Team. To prove the title Sorrow pasted three gold stars on my forehead, cut from a wallpaper sample. Once I had a queen's crown too. There are so many enjoyable uses for wallpaper samples, I wonder more people do not ask for the outdated ones.

Sorrow was sitting on the ground with her back to a tree. I walked up to her and she said, "What took you so long?"

"I had to wait for them to leave."

"Were they mad much?"

"Estie says it will be a cold day in July before she comes back," I said. "Ora said she thought you might be going through the change of life."

"I covered that five years ago," said Sorrow, sniffing. "It ain't half the hocus-pocus people make it out to be. Ora and Estie expect to be dragged off to the lunatic asylum when their time comes. Remember when we used to come out here for huckleberries, Littabelle?"

"Yes."

"And how we used to, in spring, take the flowers from these trees home and make fritters?"

"That was a long time ago."

"Eight million years."

"Eight or nine," I said.

The boughs of our overhanging tree shook down some water drops left over from the night. Under such a tree Christ was betrayed. Sorrow put her hand up to receive some of the drops, closing her fingers over them. "Littabelle, I am sick, I think."

I squatted beside her. "Where? What is it?"

"I don't mean right this minute. I mean off and on. I am sick; I know it. I think things now I never thought before. I hate. I think the world. . . . I think it might be trying to get rid of me."

"No," I said. "No."

"Don't screw your face up like that; you will have wrinkles 'fore your time. I think I am sick from the fall Hookey and I took goin' to Pintail Fork that day. When I look at myself, I look different."

"How can you look at yourself? You don't have a mirror."

"I've got the creek. It's better'n any mirror. There is something . . . something. And now I do queer things. I know I am doing them, but I cannot stop myself. Have you taken notice?"

"No." Why is it a lie always sounds louder than a truth?

"I think you might have, and I do not want to make a bigger thing of it than it has to be," said Sorrow. "The fact of the matter is, I am feelin' to myself it will get worse and I am scairt."

"I have never seen you that way," I said. I knew she was scared. I was scared. I could see fear in her eyes, not a rash spectacle. A quiet one, guiding her to duty. I felt that in some way she had gone away from me.

The rain-bearing winds in the farthest hollows swept back and forth. The sun ignited the tops of the hills. "Should you see a medical doctor?" I asked.

"I'll have no medical doctor," said Sorrow. "I know them. They use you to find out what they don't know. I'll not have one sawing my head open so's he can look inside it. I am scairt of that and I am scairt of what will happen to you and Maw Maw and Paw Paw, should I go away from you. Hutchens and Ora and Estie will not help you. They will put Maw Maw and Paw Paw away, in a old folks' home mebbe, and they will sell this land for nothing."

"They had better not try anything like that," I said. The Judas tree shook down more of its night dew.

"Maw Maw and Paw Paw . . . stay close to them. They are much like children now."

"You mustn't go away from us," I said. "The world is not trying to get rid of you."

"We must talk sensible," said Sorrow, "and not let our passions make fools of us."

"Yes, yes."

"You are choking me. Leggo. Now then, what I was leading up to was this: you are not a baby no longer. Everybody has to drop off being that when the time comes. Yours has come. Now you have got to meet your whys and wherefores face to face."

I said, "All right, I will." In that hour I would have hanged myself from the Judas tree for her. I did not know what whys and wherefores she was talking about.

"We need money to live on," said Sorrow. "When I go away from you in my mind, I won't be able to get out and do like I have."

After a while I said, "Maybe you will not go. You do not know that you will. You only think it. I do not understand what is wrong inside your head."

"I think I might've suffered some little brain bleedings," said Sorrow, looking at me straight. "And I think more will come. That day Hookey and I took our spill, I was dizzy just before it happened. Something in my head went rrrrrrrrrh, rrrrrrrrrh, and I couldn't talk to Hookey."

"You should take some Thousand-Seal," I said, referring to a herb of the aster family, an old, virtuous vulnerary used in the treatment of wounds. Its correct name is Achillea Millefolium; it is named after a Greek man named Achilles, whose mother put him and her six children in a cauldron to make them immortal. Achilles alone came out of the ordeal alive. His father saved him. I think this is a fairy tale. The Hermit at Vulture Bluff told it to me. The Hermit's real name is Winston Splitstone. Isn't that some name for you?

"Thousand-Seal will do me no good now," said Sorrow. "Listen to me. You know all my patients. Everybody knows me, knows you. Since you was a little child, they are used to seeing you come with me. You know my medicines; which is used for what."

"I want no part of any putrid colons," I said. "Or unclean livers. I don't even like to talk about intestine-flora. It makes me sick to my stomach." I could not vision myself ministering to any of Sorrow's patients. One, a woman living at Copsey Springs, birthed a new child every year along about the first or second week in November. The Hermit was the one with the unclean liver. He made his own alcoholic spirits and imbibed in them and greasy foods over-zealously.

"When you see The Hermit," said Sorrow, "tell him he can order the fresh-ground, whole-wheat flour I was talkin' to him about from a Mr. T. K. Roman down in Deaf-Smith County, Texas."

"You will tell him yourself," I said. Because I never thought I would have to go see The Hermit or the woman at Copsey Springs or any of Sorrow's patients alone. This kind of reasoning had not a leg to stand on, as you will see soon enough.

We had to abandon the work on the log house. Without Holtie there to help, it was too much. A letter from the Petifers came, saying they were being delayed in Louisiana. Holtie's brother was no better. One day I went down to their place to call on Ada's cousin. She was severely unsociable and I vowed not to go again.

General Birdwell had no work for me in his store. He also was a beekeeper and said in the spring he would furnish me an established colony in exchange for a reasonable amount of my yield. The last honey flow of the fall was over. General was requeening his colonies to assure them of young, vigorous queens to build up the hives come spring. I watched him kill one of his old queens by pinching her head off. I said to him, "That is the one part I do not like about beekeeping." General laughed.

In the forerunner of that winter, we stood in precarious straits. We butchered two of our hogs and traded the yield from one to General Birdwell for shoes, some staple food and a potbellied heating-cooking stove, which we set up in a corner of the barn loft, seating its legs on bricks, installing a flue for it and remembering to tack a sheet of asbestos on the wall in back of it. We rooted in our harvested fields and did find some potatoes, pumpkins and a few parsnips. When I reflect on the meagerness of our resources then, I wonder we did not pick up and clear out, except we are children of pioneers and pioneers ourselves and have affection for our land and know no ways other than our own. Sorrow and I fished the Rumpus River and our creek, and we canned our catch. For some of it, General Birdwell traded us jars and other necessary canning paraphernalia.

One morning we woke to hoarfrost, the ground and brown leaf all white with it. It was time for it; the Ides of October were on us. On this day the woman at Copsey Springs decided to have her eighth child, weeks before it was due. A little after noontime her oldest one came across the creek footbridge on the run, goggle-eyed and bawling for Sorrow. "Doc, Mama's about to have her baby and says for you to come quick! Quick!"

Sorrow grabbed her medical bag and she, the boy and I started out together, Sorrow on Little Boy, and the Copsey kid and I skipping alongside. After we had gone a way I turned to look at him. He was a determined little pup. I said to him, "Don't try to keep up with us. You will kill youself running."

He said, "Don't worry none about me." And we went

on. The pup knew me from other times previous, when Sorrow and I had gone to attend his mother, but we had never bothered to exchange names.

After a while Sorrow said, "Let's stop for a minute, Littabelle." We stopped, and she dismounted. The pup said, "What's the matter?"

Sorrow went over to a tree and leaned her back against it. To me she said, "You and the boy go on by yourself. I have to go back home. I am not feeling good."

"I cannot leave you here," I said. "Where don't you feel good?"

"It might be a little touch of the grippe," said Sorrow. "I am not asking you to go on with the boy; I am telling you."

The prospect of delivering the woman at Copsey Springs by myself was formidable. "I cannot go to this boy's mother and deliver her baby by myself," I said. "And I cannot leave you here by yourself."

"This is one of your wherefores," said Sorrow. "I told you you'd have to meet your whys and wherefores face to face now. You said you was willing."

"I do not know enough about delivering any baby," I said.

"You have watched me deliver this woman before," said Sorrow, and eased herself to a sitting position. "She is strong and will help you. She knows which medicines to take, and her husband will be there mebbe."

"If he is there he can do what needs to be done," I said. "Let the little pup here go on back home and tell him."

Sorrow stood up and came toward me. "Mount up, Littabelle. Let the boy ride behind you."

The pup and I mounted up. I thought I might be having a daymare. Sorrow handed me her medical kit. "I know I didn't raise no coward. The husband will pay you what he can. Best you stay the night there and come on back home tomorrow. Don't fret any about me. I am just not feeling up to snuff is all."

"If you should fall or get good and sick going back home?" I asked.

Sorrow raised her hand and smote Little Boy's flank with the palm of it. The pup put his arms around my waist to help him keep his balance. I smelled his sweat. Little Boy set himself in motion, and the pup said, "Can't this nag go no faster'n this?"

"Little Boy is no nag," I said. "You let me do the driving and just you keep your mouth shut and hang on. Is your mother in bed or what?"

"She's walking around," replied the pup. "My pa went to Vulture Bluff to see The Hermit."

"That is a good place for him," I said. "The Hermit will get him drunk, and he will be able to forget his troubles for a while. That is the way of a man. After he has caused all billy-hell trouble, he runs off to have the good time and leaves the dirty work to somebody else."

"You have a pretty neck," said the pup, thoughtful and polite. If ever I have a son, I hope he will be like that one. We got to his home at Copsey Springs, and it was strengthening and comforting to have his assistance. He directed me to wash at the pump in the yard and ordered the other children, who were standing about watching their mother pace, to gather up some food and go to the woods for the balance of the day. "Some tea," he said, organizing things. "We'd better make Mama some tea and you'd better give her some medicine."

I had brought Sorrow's medical kit into the house with me, and I opened it and looked inside. Which was used for what, that was the question. I was not able to think straight. I was barely able to remember my own name. The pup put more firewood in the stove and filled the teakettle and two large pots with water. So far, the woman had not said much to me. Every husband and father should have to watch a woman who is about to birth a new life. He would thank God every day for women. He would go down on his knees to the lowest of us. This woman was clenched deep in pain and fear. There were only three rooms to this house, so not much space to pace. Every few minutes she would sit down but would only stay in her chair a second or two. "Uhhhhh," she would say. "Uhhhhh. Ohhhhh."

I said to her, "I am trying to remember what my aunt always does for you, but isn't it funny I can't?"

"The Doc allus gives her medicine," said the pup, and pushed me out of the way and himself pawed through Sorrow's bag until he found the right one. "Here it is. This white stuff."

"Let us be doubly sure it is the right one," I said, and snatched the bottle from his hand. "You have to be careful with medicines. What if this is not the right one?"

"It's the right one," said the pup, and pried my fingers

from the bottle. "Some doctor you are. I know more'n you. You want a drink of whiskey?"

"No."

"If you faint, you will just have to stay fainted," warned the pup. "The whiskey would help, but suit yourself. I already made the room ready. As long as she'll walk, we'll let her but we got to be ready with things." He put his head back to peer at me, flint-eyed. "I guess you know now you should've been payin' more heed the times before. I used to ask myself why Doc allus brought you with her. You never did much more'n look. I bet now you wisht you had done more, don't you?"

What answer could I make to that? There wasn't one. The pup and his mother and I drank some cups of scalding tea. The pup patted his mother's hand and talked to her soothingly, "There, there. You and me has been through this before. We know it's going to be all right. It won't be long now."

The pup's mother turned her pain-blinded eyes to me. "Littabelle?"

"Ma'am?"

"Don't yell," said the pup. "She ain't deaf. She wants to go to her room now. It's time."

My God, that was some wherefore, what went on in that room that day. We only talk of our birth, we do not experience it. It is the mother who does that, and the child who turns his back on his mother should be eternally damned.

The medicine did not do much good, if any, for the pup's mother. Some pieces of burlap had been tied to the headstead of her bed, and she held on to these, pulling and straining until I thought she would break. This was strictly woman-business, and I would not let the pup come into the room. I did not see how the woman could survive the affair. She was not much bigger than I, and the violence she had to pass through was madness. There were several hours of it.

It is a confounding and shattering experience to watch a new life emerge from that of another. When you hold the new, damp form in your hands and look down at it, waiting for its first stirring, you are dumbfounded. You are stunned and excited and all the worries in your own life seem silly and little. "Hit him!" gasped the pup's mother. He was so soft and slippery, I almost dropped him. I hit him on his hindsides, and the air rushed into his lungs. He let out his first scream. I felt his hand on my wrist.

I went out the window and buried the afterbirth in the yard. It was hard work digging the hole for it. The pup did not come out with any offer to help; I did not ask for any help. When I had got his mother and the new one cleaned up and settled, I went out to the living part of the house and said to him, "Well, you have got another brother. What do you think about that?"

He had been sweeping the floor but now rested his broom. "You got blood on you," he observed.

I said, "Dear God, is that all you've got to say to me?"

"The Doc allus gets a drink of whiskey afterward. You want one?"

"No."

"You look like you might could use one."

"I have never touched alcohol," I said. "Why do you want me to now?"

"You want to sit down?" asked the pup, sympathetic.

"I had better," I said.

The pup picked up a chair, brought it over and set it down in front of me. I sat. The pup went to a cabinet, unscrewed the lid of a jar, took out three dollars and came back to me. "Pa said to give this to Doc Sorrow, but he didn't know the Doc herself wouldn't come. This is how much he allus pays."

I said, "Well, this is a caution if I ever saw one. Do you mean to tell me this is all your father pays my aunt to be midwife to your mother?"

The pup held his broom again. Shrewdly, he said, "Seems like a-plenty to me. I wisht I could earn three dollars."

"Pup," I said, "how old are you?"

"Twelve," he replied. "And my name's not Pup." He was fair and had an obstinate chin and mouth. The three bills in my hand were turning me angry; they were so pitifully little and were the declarations of one whole life-time—Sorrow's. If ever I had entertained any romantic notion of taking Sorrow's place among the people of the region, it left me then.

I felt sorry for the pup, for he was the eldest of many, and already his mother was overaged from overwork and too-frequent childbearing. Some Ozark people tend to lose their teeth early, and the pup's mother had. I said to him, "Well, if your name is not Pup what is it? Josephine?"

The pup could take a joke. "Josephine is the one next down from me. And then there's Vaseline and then Kerosene. You can call me Pup if you want. It's as good a name as any."

Leaving Pup to his sweeping, I went outside to the pump place and cleaned myself up. There was soap there and a crash towel. The wind was kicking up a little; there were drifts of fog among the trees. As I was finishing my toilet, Pup's father came through the trees. The Hermit was with him. Both had been drinking. They came ambling up to me, and I said to Pup's father, "You have a new son."

"Lord have mercy," said Pup's father, as if I had just sprung something unexpected on him. He went shuffling into his house, and The Hermit made himself comfortable on the woodpile. "I have had a day," he commented.

"You look it," I said. "If your eyes were any redder, you could use them for lamps."

"Where is Sorrow?" asked Winston Splitstone, The Hermit.

"Sick."

"How so?"

"Are you so drunk you cannot understand English? Sorrow is sick."

"I am not drunk," said The Hermit. "I never get drunk. I only drink. I am what is known as a still-drunk. What is wrong with Sorrow?"

"I do not know. Maybe she has the grippe. She is not feeling good, that is all."

The Hermit eyed me. "Is that what you're mad about?"

"People should have more respect for their mothers," I said.

"Right so," said The Hermit.

"Anybody doesn't have respect for his mother and refuses to do for her should be locked up in jail."

"Right so," said The Hermit.

"And people should have more respect for doctors too. You know how much I got paid for my work today? Three dollars."

The Hermit sometimes affected talking like one of us because he wanted to be. "Wal," he said, "that ain't the most money in the world but it ain't the least neither. In anybody's language three dollars is three dollars. You think it'll snow? You feel that wind? It's a-comin', the snow is."

"I have got a new principle," I said.

"That is a strange word to hear coming from your lips," said The Hermit. "Aren't you about through washing there? You are going to wash yourself away."

"I have got a new principle and it is this," I said. "If the club you are carrying isn't big enough, go get yourself another one."

"Right so," said The Hermit.

CHAPTER SIX

I can tell you this for a certainty: Wit may be born with man and sense too, but he has got to be allowed the time to dawdle and doodle and send his mind on excurions, else he will wind up with a bundle of faggots. Teachers should take a second look at teaching. I am certain many heroes and saints, inventors and great world investigators have been lost in classrooms because of teachers who only thunder instruction every minute.

It was General Birdwell who decided me I should become a teacher. The day after my ordeal at Copsey Springs, General came up from Pioneer Gap to notify Paw Paw he had sold his store to a man from Okolona. He was out trying to liquidate some of the debt standing on his books. It hurt me to hear Paw Paw's shamed honesty. "General," he said, "today I couldn't buy gold bricks, two for a nickel."

"I hated like sin to come up here and dun you," said General. "Ye Gods, are you actually livin' in this loft?"

"Our Lord Jesus was born in a barn," said Paw Paw.

"True," admitted General, solemn as a sinner after committing his deed. "But ye Gods, man, times have changed. Do Hutchens and Ora and Estie know you're livin' like this?"

"They know it, and they're givin' what help they can," said Paw Paw. "You got a tally on how much I owe you, General?"

"Three-hundred and twenty-seven dollars," said General. "It's been addin' up for several years, like you know. I hated like sin to come up here and dun you for it. I thought mebbe Hutchens might be giving you a little aid. Or Ora or Estie. If the debt has to stay on the books, the new owner will charge interest. That's the way he works. He has got two bird dogs down at the store now, countin' every nail and weighin' every pound to see if I have cheated him on the inventory. I have bent backwards to give him a fair deal."

"I don't imagine you would be willing to wipe off some of what I owe you in trade for some acreage?" asked Paw Paw.

"No," replied General. "I am land poor." He and Paw Paw were old friends and he felt bad about the meeting, though no worse than Paw Paw.

Sorrow had viewed the proceeding with scarcely a word. She had got up that morning with an ambition to make sauerkraut but lacked the main ingredient. "To not even have a cabbage to your name," she said. "It's awful, and nobody cares. We are all going to die here in this barn this winter. You hear that wind a-whistlin'? You feel that cold a-comin'? We are all going to freeze to death in our beds when the worst of it gets here."

"Hush," I said. "Hush. None of us is going to die anywhere. Not any time soon anyway. I have decided to become a schoolkeeper, and I am going over to Pintail Fork now to see Merlie Bud Luckabill about giving me the examination for the work. Do I look all right to go?"

"You are a charm in that outfit," said Sorrow. I had on the yellow dress with the neck-to-hem ruffle and over it a black surtout undoubtedly inherited by Holtie from a better-off relative. It had a velvet collar and was lined with fleece. I had had a taste of meeting one of my wherefores, and the three dollars I had got for it had been a revelation. Beware of the one newly awakened and angered to action. He might be a dark horse.

Sorrow did not have a touch of the grippe, as she had claimed the day prior. Now is as good a time as any to tell you about Maw Maw and Paw Paw's attitude toward her condition during this time. To tote it up: Old age shrinks from change and will sometimes deny its presence. For it, yesterday is today. It has not the time left nor the strength to oppose new currents and apply remedies.

Maw Maw gave me a package of brown eggs to take

as a gift to the Luckabills. I said to her, "I will try to be back before dark, but if it gets late too soon I will stay over until tomorrow morning. Watch yourselves while I am gone."

"Don't worry none about us," said Maw Maw. Oh, she was the valiant one.

I cannot tell you how many miles it is from Blue Ash Hollow to Pintail Fork. Distances in this region are not counted by miles or rods. The mountaineer counts the number of curves in his road or trail and will say it was that many or that many curves from here to there. Well, Little Boy and I did not take any roads that day because, as I have told you before, there were not any.

We crossed the creek and started up through the woods, pushing along at a fair clip. There was a stable chill in the air; the temperature might have stood at forty degrees. Little Boy was a reliable traveler. Between us we chose the easier trails. The vales and rain-glens offered galore their seasonal shows of color. Life in them was quieting; it would grow quieter with the advance of winter.

We passed by little side hollows, and out one of these silently stepped The Hermit and Pup from Copsey Springs. Their appearance startled Little Boy, and he started to bolt. Reining him in, I said, "You should give some notice before you step out in somebody's path that way. Have you ever been kicked by a scared burro?"

"No," replied The Hermit. "That's one experience I've missed."

Pup held up a white, waxy looking clump. "Look. Mistletoe."

I said to The Hermit, "If you were a gentleman, you would turn your head so I could get down and stretch my legs. This fool dress I've got on was not made for this kind of traveling."

The Hermit and Pup obligingly turned their heads and I, with some difficulty, dismounted. I wonder what fool thought of the idea of putting women in skirts. There is so much wasted material in them and they do not allow us to move about as freely as we could in trousers. The skirt of my yellow dress was wrinkled. I said to The Hermit, "I am on my way to Pintail Fork to see Merlie Bud Luckabill about taking the examination to teach the school there. He has varicose veins and often needs a deputy to stand in. I don't suppose you know anything about it?"

"About school-keeping examinations?" said The Hermit. "Wal, I've never been no teacher but I've read a few books in my time. What do you think you'd like to know?"

I said, "If I knew what I thought I wanted to know, I would know it."

"Don't be sassy with me," said The Hermit. "I am not here to do you any favors. If you want to sit down here on this log with Pup and me and discuss your problem in a reasonable way, we will do it, and I will try to advise you but I will not put up with no ugly manners."

I unbuttoned Holtie's surtout and we sat on the log, Pup being careful not to crush his mistletoe clump. I said, "Well, to begin with, I do not know what I would like to know because I cannot think what questions will be on Merlie Bud's examination."

"The school at Pintail Fork has grades from one through eight," said The Hermit. "I should think subjects like arithmetic and history and geography would be taught."

"When Mama don't need me at home and it's not too cold, I go there," said Pup. "When Mr. Luckabill is teacher, he just hollers all day long and fights with us. We don't learn nothin' from him. When L. C.'s teacher, we go on field trips."

The Hermit said to me, "Can you name the states in our Union?"

"Sure."

"Do it then."

"Arkansas. Oklahoma. Louisiana. Canada."

The Hermit put one of his hands over his face. "Hoooeee!"

"That's not right?"

"Canada is not one of our states, Missy."

"It isn't? Well, you have got to understand when I was a pupil I did not think I would ever want to be a teacher."

"That has got nothing to do with the price of cotton in Natchez," said The Hermit. "I never wanted to be a teacher either, but when I went to school I blamed sure learned the names of all the states in our Union. Their capitals, too."

"I was not a good pupil. I always wanted to be some-place else. Now I could kick myself. Why didn't I look ahead to this? Why didn't I pay attention and learn like I was supposed to?"

"I don't know," answered The Hermit. "How much do you know about the multiplication tables?"

"I know them all. I have had twelve years of schooling."

"If that is so," said The Hermit, "you must have started when you was four. Ain't you only sixteen now?"

"Yes. I started school when I was six."

"Six plus twelve is eighteen," said The Hermit.

"I know it. I skipped a couple of grades. Do not think I am dumb just because I thought Canada was one of our states. I am not. A couple of my teachers did not think so anyway. There are more ways than one to being smart. Because I am so runty I had to spend a lot of my time fighting when I was in school. Think about that a while."

"I will when I get time," murmured The Hermit.

The day was running on, and I was getting nothing of any use from the conversation. I stood up and prepared to be on my way, flexing my legs another time and buttoning the surtout. The Hermit, who could show some manners when it pleased him, stood up also. Pup remained silently seated on the log. The Hermit said, "Littabelle, where did you get the idea you wanted to teach school?"

"I delivered Pup's mother for three dollars," I said, "and it nearly killed us both. I do not want to spend my life like Sorrow has spent hers. We have been burned out and are having to live in our barn. General Birdwell has sold his store to a man from Okolona and we owe him three-hundred and twenty-seven dollars, not counting the interest he will add. If I get the school-teaching job at Pintail Fork, how much do you think it will pay?"

"I should think Merlie Bud might draw fifty or sixty dollars a month," answered Winston Splitstone, The Hermit. "So if he was to hire you to stand in for him for, say a week, you could reasonably expect to draw one fourth of that."

"How much is one fourth of sixty?"

"Littabelle," said The Hermit. "You don't want to teach school. There are some people just aren't suited to it."

"I am not a baby any more to have everything suited to me. Tending to the sick is not suited to me. Besides that, it does not pay for shoe leather. Besides that, how people are arranged inside turns my stomach."

"If you know how people are arranged inside, you are one up on me," said The Hermit. "It is all I can do to keep up with how they are arranged on the outside. Even then, I sometimes have my doubts."

"I know where everything in the human body is," I said. "Every vein and organ and nerve. Sorrow taught me from a book. And Paw Paw. When you butcher, you have to know these things. People are not arranged much different from animals inside."

"They are less pleasantly arranged than animals from the outside," observed The Hermit.

Little Boy and I got to Merlie Bud's school a few minutes after the time his noon recess was over, only it was not Merlie Bud who was calling the shots that day. It was his grandboy, L. C. The building looked as if it was ready to call it quits, a faded, one-room affair standing lonesome in a yard that was a lawless mess of dirty paper scraps, fruit cores and peelings and otherwise-trash. I led Little Boy around to the back of the building and tethered him in a place where the wind would not hit him broad-blast.

L. C. spied me from one of the windows and came outside. I told him I was there to see Merlie Bud, and he said his grandfather was home sick with tonsillitis. I told him I had come to Pintail Fork to see Merlie Bud about taking the school-keeping examination, and he brightened and suggested I go back inside with him for a look at the facilities. The wind was picking up with some real authority, and the sky was graying.

There were fifteen children of this school and all greeted me with great, gritty looks. I thought of how I must look to them, a peaky-looking girl in a man's overcoat. I was sorry I had not cut my hair or at least put it up. I thought I was in an enemy camp, and I wondered how I would go about handling the foe were I given the chance to try.

L. C. and I reached his teaching desk, which was at the head of the room, without incident. Underneath the desk there were lunch boxes and stacks of books. On top of the desk there was one lunch box, more books, a long ruler, a knife with an open blade, a pencil box and a fountain pen. Behind the desk there was the blackboard. L. C.'s little spyglass gillie, Salem Cayce, was at the board writing SILENCE IS GOLDEN. The board was covered with this saying but he was out to do even a better job. His lip was in his teeth and he was mad. He walked back and forth in front of the board looking for bare spaces to write in and he found them, scrawling in the margins and between the lines, SILENCE IS GOLDEN. L. C. said to him, "Awright, you can quit now."

"I'm not finished," said Salem. He skipped around L. C. and me, located another vacant space and wrote little letters between the big ones. SILENCE IS GOLDEN.

"I said you could quit," said L. C. Now the three of us standing at the head of the room had the attention of all the others in it. They smiled at me but not in friendliness. There were a couple of handsome ones. They all looked bored and tough, even the girls. I thought of my own days in school. I had been tough.

One kid at the back of the room had drawn himself an extra pair of eyes on his forehead. Another had his shoes and socks off, had his feet up on his desk and was picking his toes. He was big and thickset. Boy, I thought. Oh, boy.

L. C. invited me to sit in his teacher's chair and I did. The room was hot and close, not a window opened for ventilation. The heat was coming from a cast-iron stove set in the center of the room.

L. C. spoke again to Salem. "I said you could quit now. Go on back to your desk and set there and don't open your mouth till I tell you to."

What happened then goes past common belief, but it is the Lord's truth and I tell it without any dressings. Salem threw his hands up and pitched his stick of chalk out over the heads of the pupils. I did not hear it land, and I remember thinking I should have because the floor was hard and bare and there were no shufflings or coughings or snickerings.

"Go get the chalk, Salem," said L. C., "and bring it back up here to me."

Salem stepped away from the blackboard and started

to swagger-walk down between the rows of desks, dragging his heels, grinning down into the faces upturned to his, enjoying himself. To his classmates he was a hero in some sense. Whatever victory was at stake, it was going to be his. I thought he was a little ruffian, a mischiefmaker, and I began to have some second thoughts about my mission there.

L. C. was standing stiff beside my chair watching Salem, who was only making a token pretense to look for the piece of chalk. Beside the desk of the barefoot boy he got down of all fours and peered. "Where's my chalk? Anybody seen it?"

Somebody said, "Royce has got it. He's eatin' it. He's hongry."

Salem went toward the kid with the extra pair of eyes painted on his forehead. "Royce, gimme my chalk. L. C. wants it. You know you ain't supposed to eat it. You been told a hundred times."

The big, barefoot boy stood up and moved out into the aisle to stand in back of Salem. I could not see Royce Fredericks. There was a bucket of water on top of the stove and it was steaming.

"Hey, hey," somebody said. It was Salem, stepping back from Royce and half-turning toward L. C. and me. In the space between Salem and the barefoot one, I saw Royce slip from his seat to the floor. He had his hands around his throat. Something bad was happening to him. At first I did not see it as bad; I thought it was a monkeyshine and so did L. C. He said, "Royce, get up off that floor and set in your seat. Salem, go to your desk. And Idus, you go to yours."

Idus, the barefoot one, leaned to Royce. "Hey, boy, what's the matter with you? You sick?"

All of the children were now standing in the aisles, craning their heads for a look at Royce. There was a queer lack of excitement in all of this. I think mountain children do not act in emergency as children of towns do. There is something old in them. Salem said, "L. C., you better come here. I think ol' Royce is chokin' to death."

"What the heck now," said L. C., and he and I ran down the aisle to Royce. He was still on the floor with his legs in the air, and he was pumping them. There was a tide of red in his face. He had his mouth open, trying to pull air into his lungs. His pair of artificial eyes was puckered; his natural ones were bugged out of his head and swimming in tears. L. C. yanked him to his feet and started pummeling him on the back. All of this was a desperate thing to see. One time I had witnessed a dog belonging to one of Sorrow's patients come near to death in the same fix. With the help of its owner and myself, Sorrow saved it.

"This'll teach you," said L. C., shaking Royce like a rag. "I told you and told you not to eat chalk. Spit it out!"

Royce could not obey. He was actually choking to death before our very eyes.

Who knows about courage until he has it? If, in that moment, mine came from reason, I did not know sicum about it. What it boiled down to was, I saw the danger and I did not stop to think if L. C. saw it or could do anything about it himself. When you see danger, you either run backward from it or forward to it. Usually it will come too fast to do any reasoning about it. From the stove and from the bodies pressed close around I smelled the stale heat in the room, and between determination and disbelief in what I could do, I said to L. C., "Put him down. And somebody give me some books to put under him."

L. C. said, "What? What?" He lowered Royce to the floor. Royce was still jerking and clawing but not so energetically as before. The red in his face had begun to drain, giving way to a chilly blue color. I thought he was dying. I knew he would die and would not be long about it unless some severe action was taken at once. I bent to him and took his face in my hands. His mouth was open; I pried it open yet wider and peered in. I could not see the piece of chalk that was causing all the trouble. It is lodged in his gullet, I thought.

Salem was beside me, thrusting a pile of books at me. I directed L. C. and Idus and Salem. "Get these books under his shoulder blades. I want him so his head will fall back. Somebody sit on his feet. One of you get over in back of him and hold his shoulders. I am going to try and save his life but it will be tricky. I do not want him to jerk when I stick him with the knife."

"Knife!" exclaimed L. C., less calm than any of the children. His face was as white as flour.

I ran back up the aisle to L. C.'s deak and grabbed the knife lying there and the fountain pen. There was a back door to the room and I actually thought of using it. The wind was making the building creak, and I thought of

Little Boy out in it, probably shivering. On the way back to Royce I shed Holtie's overcoat. I knelt on one side of Royce, and I thought he was gone. The whole thing was real and believable, and yet it was unreal and unbelievable. I could not look at Royce's face. I could not think of my actions. I only acted. The fool dress with the ruffle and too much material in its skirt was hampering me. I yanked it up over my knees and straddled Royce. It was the wrong position. Maybe. There was no time to take up another. I leaned to Royce's throat. The collar around it had been pulled away. The throat loomed big in my eyes, a huge, slightly dirty stalk, white against the blue collar. It blurred in my vision and shrunk. Lord. I said to Salem who was rubbering me hard, "You want to do this? All right, shut up then."

"I didn't say nothin'," said Salem.

"Just shut up. Get somebody else to hold his shoulders down. You hold his head. Put one hand on either side of his head and hold it. I want his neck up. Up! Hold his head! Pull on it!"

Salem breathed, "Do it, lady, if you're going to." He had Royce's head in both of his hands and was pulling back on it. Royce's neck was arched upward. He is dead, I thought, and I put the point of the knife against his throat a little below his Adam's apple. Where was my courage? The wind creaked the building. Salem's eyes on me were adrift in pools of great friendliness and wonderment. I thought—What if this was me instead of Royce? And I thought—Which way to go? Up or down? Back or forth? Which was it when I helped Sorrow save that dog?

I did not think I could do it. I did it. I took a grip on the handle of the knife and put the point of it into the skin of Royce's neck and made a bold, vertical cut. He did not scream for he was nearer death than life and anyway it takes breath to scream and he did not have any to spare. Idus was sitting on Royce's legs. Probably breaking them, I thought. I thought the blood coming from Royce's neck was too red and there was too much of it. I wondered if I might have cut his jugular vein. I heard the creak of the wind against the building. There was the windpipe. Encircled with rings of cartilage. Should I cut between the rings? Yes. The chalk had to be lodged in the throat above the windpipe. The thing to do was make a little hole in the pipe and then stick something in it to keep it open. Royce could breathe through the hole; his lungs could get air that way. Worry about the chalk later. Somebody else could take that out. A doctor. . . . Make the hole.

I made the hole. I heard Royce suck air through it, one of the best sounds I had ever heard. I thought I spoke calmly to a female face hanging over one of my shoulders. "You see that fountain pen there on the floor by my foot? There is a little rubber tube in it. Take it out of the pen and throw it away. Yank it out. Then cut off the other end of the holder. Oh, here. Give it to me, fumble-fingers."

L. C. said, "What're you doing?"

I said, "What do you care? He is breathing, isn't he? I am putting this tube in his throat so he can breathe through it and stay alive until somebody can get him to a doctor. I need something I can use to bind the tube to his throat.

Do you have anything?"

L. C. could not think of what could be used for a bandage. I had Salem rip the ruffle from my dress for that purpose. He said, "You did good, lady. You did real good."

Royce lay on the floor with Holtie's surtout over him until his mother and father came. I told them they should take their son to a medical doctor, and they said, "Yes, Ma'am." It was the first time anybody had ever called me that. Ma'am.

After that I got the job to be deputy schoolkeeper at Pintail Fork.

CHAPTER SEVEN

In the rhubarbs of Arkansas, education was not the most lusted-after commodity at that time. I can think that the state established the school at Pintail Fork, agreed to pay someone to give and hear lessons, then departed the scene, leaving it to be the makeshift agency it was, generally lifeless and marked by lack of acquaintance with outside ministering. During the time I was keeper there, I never saw anybody from the state.

Merlie Bud gave me the examination for the job the afternoon of the Royce Fredericks incident. He was sick, and the kids who followed L. C. and me from the school building to his house were noisy outside so we got through with it quickly. The kids took up positions on Merlie Bud's porch and stared in at us through the windows. Peevish, Merlie Bud said, "What're they doing out there? What're they so worked up about?"

L. C. said, "But Grandpa, I told you. Littabelle just saved the life of little Royce Fredericks. He was chokin' to death on a piece of chalk, and she cut a hole in his neck and saved his life. Idus, Salem and me helped her. Idus sat on his legs—"

"I'm fevered," interrupted Merlie Bud, "and don't want to hear it again." He had his throat doctored with some kind of healing oil and swathed in cotton batting fastened on one side with a big safety pin. I doubt if he was authorized or qualified to give the school-keeping examination to any applicant. He asked me to read aloud to him two pages from a textbook and demonstrate that I could write cursive. Then I did some arithmetic problems and spelled some words for him. I recall three of them; *judgment* and *especially* and *tongue*. I thought they were tricky. When I had finished with that, Merlie Bud coughed and said, "When Royce gets back to school, try to keep the chalk away from him."

"I said, "You mean you are giving me the job?"

"You are the only applicant for it. L. C. don't want it any more. He's got bees in his pants to get to the woods and make hisself some money guiding parties who don't know the difference between a rabbit and a man-eatin' panther."

"Yes," agreed L. C., "I'll be doing that off and on all

winter now. But I'll be here some off and on too."

I said, "Merlie Bud, when do you want me to start?"

Merlie Bud said, "Take into consideration today is Friday. There won't be any more school till Monday. You can start then."

"How long can I count on this time?"

"Two weeks," answered Merlie Bud. "I get this stuff every year about this time, and it allus hangs on at least two weeks. Sometimes longer. You come Monday and be prepared to stay two weeks. You can board and room with us if you want or you can go home every day soon as school's out. Work it whichever way you want."

"How much do you charge for board and room?" I asked.

"Two dollars for five days," said Merlie Bud.

"Even if the days are sprinkled out?"

"It don't differ," said Merlie Bud. "Work it whichever way you want."

"What will the salary be?"

Merlie Bud took a figure from his head. "Seven dollars for five days." I thought he was cutting me off at the pockets a little but did not argue with him about it.

Dovie invited me to stay that night with them, but I was excited and declined the offer. I was anxious to get home and tell Sorrow and Maw Maw and Paw Paw about my job. Salem Cayce, Idus and their pals accompanied L. C. and me back to the schoolhouse where I had left Little Boy. The wind had calmed somewhat. It had commenced to mist. Salem asked if I would not like to go to his house for supper. I said, "No, I am afraid you might poison me. I am going to be your teacher come next Monday morning."

"No," he said. "I wouldn't poison you. You and me is buddies. Yessir."

On his mount, a pretty little fawn-colored pony named Edna, L. C. rode part of the way to Blue Ash Hollow with me. When he told me his animal's name, I said a silly thing. "I'll bet Edna is the name of some girl you like."

His reply was, "Edna is my mother's name." He sure loved Edna. We stopped by his house for a minute because he wanted to exchange his light wrap for a heavier one, and I saw his mother. She was in her backyard chopping wood. L. C. got down from his pony and went over to his mother and took the axe out of her hand. "Mama, when you get short on wood for the house you should tell me. You look cold. Go inside."

"That girl," said L. C.'s mother, looking across the yard to Little Boy and me. "She the one performed the operation on Royce Fredericks?"

"Yes," replied L. C.

"How do," said L. C.'s mother, inspecting me. "I didn't get your name."

"It's Littabelle Lee."

"You any kin to Sorrow Lee?"

"She is my aunt."

"If you come out half the woman Sorrow is, you will be all right," said L. C.'s mother. She did not ask me in to her house. She was a grass widow. When L. C. was twelve, his father rode off in the direction of Missouri one day and never came back. To hear the account of a disappeared person is always unsettling because it argues of desperate steps, whether willing or unwilling.

I wanted to get going and so did Little Boy. We did not need L. C. to escort us from town. Still, we waited there in the mist and the rumoring wind while he chopped enough wood to last at least three days. I thought he worked a little too proud for such a scrubby audience. There is something about a boy showing off his manhood that comes off a little tacky, and yet you have to see the grace in this too.

I compared L. C. to Hutchens. I had never seen Hutchens relieve Maw Maw of any chore or even a piece of one. He, like Estie and Ora, was always the guest when he came. I will tell you this about those three: I had begun to grow a pretty strapping dislike for them. When you are a child, you forgive visitors their lack of manners because you know you are not any part of them and they will go away come nightfall. They are temporary and they take their lack of compassion with them when they go. In my childhood I never hated Hutchens or Ora or Estie or even disliked them very much. Now it was different because I had left off being a child and was feeling things I had not felt.

L. C. escorted me three quarters of the way to Blue Ash Hollow that day, though I kept telling him he should turn back. He laid out a trail he said I should follow going to and fro from Pintail Fork to Blue Ash Hollow. "And you should always wear something red on your head to let hunters know you aren't a wild animal. They ain't always choosey picking what to shoot at."

"No hunter had better take any pot shot at me," I said. "If he does, he will find himself pushing up daisies."

"That is big talk for a girl," said L. C.

"If you think I would let anybody pick me off out here in the woods, you are crazy. I would not let anybody pick me off anywhere. I would be the one to shoot first and ask the questions afterward."

"I will tell you when a man is in the woods with a gun lookin' for animals to kill he ain't nice," said L. C.

"Any man who would kill an animal just for the sport of it cannot be nice anywhere," I said.

"You are a gutty girl."

"Gutty? Oh, I do not think so. I only use what sense I've got. I enjoy doing that."

"Maybe you are too gutty. A man don't like to look at a girl too gutty."

I said, "I do not see any man around here, but even if I did I would not change myself for him."

"A man who's been in the woods three or four days with other men ain't hisself," said L. C. "He goes crazy. He does things he wouldn't think of doin' at home. The woods ain't safe for a girl during hunting season."

"You were the one to put in my mind I should try for the job at Pintail Fork," I pointed out.

"I didn't know you then," said L. C.

"You do not know me now," I retorted. We only went another yard or two more together. Then L. C., showing a little pique for a reason lost on me, turned his mount around and whirled away through the trees and mist. It started to rain.

For two days we saw nothing but black rain. The barn loft was cold and drafty. We were obliged to keep a fire in the potbellied stove all the time and the roof over the bed Paw Paw and Maw Maw shared sprang a leak. Paw Paw and I brought ladders from the lower half of the barn, climbed up, and did the best we could toward repairing it. It was a job. Sorrow would not help or show any interest in the problem. She sat idle by the stove, talking, talking about her girlhood, laughing to speak again of Jean Ladeau, the Frenchman who escaped from her and died of a liver disease among his Indian friends on the banks of the Rumpus River. Then she would switch and speak of Hutchens, Ora and Estie, bitter-tonguing them for every lack and failure. During one of these screeds she voiced a yearning to see her friend, The Hermit, and when next there came a lull in the rain, snatched a shawl from Ada Petifer's clothing box and bounded out. The three of us remaining watched her jump the puddles in the yard and scurry across the footbridge. Just as she reached the farthest end of it, the rain began again, closing her to our vision. I wanted to go after her and bring her back but Maw Maw said, "No, let her go. She'll come back of her own accord when she's ready."

That is the day Sorrow took up residence with Winston Splitstone. When the evening had come, he came to tell us that she had. "She wants to live with me now."

"When will you marry?" asked Paw Paw.

Wet and gloomy, The Hermit met Paw Paw's gaze direct. "We haven't talked about marriage."

" 'Twouldn't be right, her to live with you without

marriage," said Paw Paw.

Said The Hermit, "I am not against marrying your daughter. But I don't want to talk to her about that now. She is sick."

"We know," said Maw Maw.

"She came to me and asked to live with me," said The Hermit, "and I said yes. She feels protected in my house. Would you have me turn her out? We will talk about marriage when the time is better." In a valise he had brought he took most of Sorrow's things back to Vulture Bluff with him but not her medical bag or any of her medicines. He said Sorrow had voiced to him her intention to give up her practice. I will tell you this was a bad thing to happen to my grandparents. I would like to say my own thoughts concerning this turn of events were only glad ones for Sorrow. I cannot. I thought also of what her going would mean to the three of us left in the barn. However flit and drag the money from her practice had been, it was now no more. I tell you life is a warfare. You had better learn early to take up the cudgel.

The next morning Maw Maw and I set up a little workshop near the stove and attempted to lay out a school wardrobe for me. We had Maw Maw's tin sewing box, blackened from the fire, but the inside contents were not damaged. We shortened the yellow dress and with the leftover material made a new ruffle for it. We paired a black skirt from Ada Petifer's box with a khaki shirt of Holtie's, aiming for an outfit that would lend me a military bearing. We cut a pair of divided riding pants from the skirt that would look like a skirt when the legs it would cover were in a normal, ladylike position. For quite a few hours we bent to this task. Off and on, the pants were either too skinny or too generous. Vexed at one point, Maw Maw said, "Sorrow should be here. I do believe I've forgotten what little bit I ever knew about this. Oh, Littabelle, what is happening to Sorrow? What's wrong with her, do you think?"

"She is catching up with some things she has missed," I said. "That's all. We should not worry about her. She is where she wants to be. The Hermit is a good man. He is her good friend. He will not let any harm come to her."

With her mouth full of pins, Maw Maw said, "When Hutchens and Ora and Estie come we won't tell them where Sorrow is. We will just say she is off in the hills tending to one of her patients. Unless she and Mr. Splitstone marry meantime."

"Yes, if they come we will say that," I said. When pressed with a sadiron, the articles of my work wardrobe were improved. For our supper that night we had a jar of our home-preserved fish and fried parsnips.

Little Boy and I left home before daybreak the next morning. The rain had quit, and there had been a drop in the temperature. We traveled in the light of the moon and the stars and, except for the sounds we ourselves made, the forest was deeply still. We did not see or hear any hunters, but as we by-passed one hollow we saw the scatter-pother of where a party of them had camped. What a disgraceful mess of fire-scorch, condiment jars, paper rubbish and evidence of Sir John Barleycorn. And speared on a stick set in the ground, the body of a bloated, decaying rabbit. What paladins and men of fine mettle those must have been. It was my impulse to dismount and bury the little animal, but I had no digging tool with me, only Holtie's Petifer's carbine.

By the time I got to Pintail Fork, the residents of the town were up and stirring. I could see them moving about through the windows of their lighted houses and thought I could smell their coffee and bacon. We went through the town and around a hill to the schoolhouse. Salem Cayce was there ahead of me, sitting on the steps with his arms folded. He called out a queer greeting. "The best of the day to you."

I said, "Hey," and rode Little Boy around to the back of the building and tethered him there to an elm tree. I had brought along some corn and a bucket for his drinking water. Salem took the vessel from me, trotted over to an outside spigot, filled it and returned with it. Little Boy started his breakfast, and Salem and I went inside.

"L. C. brought you a clock," said Salem, pointing to one on the teacher's desk. "And told me to help you get started. In fifteen minutes I'll start ringin' the bell. By that time most everybody should be here. They should line up outside and they shouldn't talk. I'll tell them to shut up if you don't want to."

I said, "No, I'll tell them to shut up. I'm the teacher."

"I like them pants you got on," said Salem. "Don't be scairt. I'm going to help you. At eight o'clock, on the dot, everybody should come inside. They should march in.

They should sing while they're marchin' in. You know any marching songs?"

"I might know a couple, but offhand I can't think what they are," I replied. "I whistle better than I sing."

"Never mind," said Salem. "We got a Victrola. L. C. loaned it 'cause he knew you wouldn't know how to sing."

"L. C. knows so much he should go to Washington city and be President," I said. "Where is the cloakroom?"

"There," answered Salem, pointing to a door. "I built a fire already. L. C. told me I should. He said for me to tell you about the toilets, too. They're out back. The one with the pink door is the one for the girls, and the one with the blue door is the one for the boys. L. C. and me painted them that way because everybody was always getting them mixed up and going in the wrong one. You think L. C. is good-lookin'?"

"No."

"Here's the roll book. After we say the pledge of allegiance to the flag and say prayer and sing a song, everybody should sit down. Then you call the roll and then you can get started. L. C. told me I should move my desk up here. It used to belong to Ruth Porter, but L. C. told me to switch with her so I could sit up here close to you and help out."

Well, it is a strain on my memory to remember how I got that job started, and there might be some mercy in this. After the marching in and the saying of the pledge of allegiance to the flag, then a prayer and then a song with a voice on the Victrola leading, there came a pause in occupation. Then I called the roll. Then Salem's hand shot up and I granted him permission to come to my desk and be my assistant. We instructed everybody to open their books and have a study period. We got a six- and seven-year-old brother and sister, named Doris and Dowling, started with alphabet blocks and molding clay. They didn't want to learn the alphabet or make clay animals. They wanted to fight over who should occupy the greater portion of the seat they were required to share. So I gave Salem L. C.'s knife, which had been left in the teaching desk, and told him to go outside and cut two switches from a tree. While this was being done, Doris bit Dowling and he punched her in the stomach with his fist. Doris then took up a wad of her clay, set it on Dowling's head and pounded it to a flat cake. Salem came back with the switches, and I took Doris and Dowling to the cloakroom, handed each a switch and told them to go to it. They backed away, embarrassed. I dragged them together again. "You want to kill each other, don't you? Well, go ahead. I give you my permission. This is your golden chance."

"I don't like you," said Dowling. "Even if you did save Royce Fredericks' life. I don't want you for my teacher."

"It is not what you want that makes you fat," I said. "Fight."

"I will tell my mama on you," said Doris, and with her switch laid a stinging blow across the backs of my legs. I grabbed her up and thrust her at Dowling. "Swack her! Punch her in the stomach! Gouge her eyes out! Now is your chance! You will never get another, I promise you."

"You leave my sister alone," bawled Dowling, and with

his head lowered rushed me. He knocked both Doris and me to the floor. It was not a clean fracas where everybody got up and shook hands afterward.

Doris and Dowling were two kids I could feel religious about in a way somewhat beyond my explaining. They were over-serious. The world bemused them, and yet made them querulous. One time I wanted Doris to be the White Dove of Peace in a school play, but the mother of these two slick-eyed dandiprats said no. I asked her why, and she said, "Would you put a white dress on a bulldog and try to make people believe he was a little bird?"

Ruth Porter was my second-grader. She wore enormous hair bows and aprons. On my order she stood beside her desk, chewing her fingers. We were not prepared for each other. "Speak," I said.

"Speak what?" asked Ruth, bending her legs at the knees.

"Speak your lesson."

"I don't have no lesson. I didn't get one 'cause L. C. forgot me."

"Sit down then and study your book."

"What page?"

How should I know? "Page seventeen."

"Seventeen?" Still with her legs bent at the knees and with her hair bow bobbing under the weight of anxiety, Ruth leaned to her desk, took up a book, pawed through the pages. "I don't see—"

"Can't you find page seventeen?"

"In a minute. I think. . . . No, that's too many. Let me

start over. One, two, three, four, five—"

"Ruth, just turn to page seventeen. It'll be printed on the corner. You'll see it."

Some more frantic pawing and Idus, in the sixth-grade section, stealthily removing his shoes and long, black socks. Watching me from under his eyelids. Slowly he brought one of his legs up to rest on the opposite knee. Bent to his foot. What was he searching for? Ah, there. Toe-jam. What heaven. O, Idus, what a lunk you are. You smell like a barnyard. If you have a brain growing in your head, you do a good job hiding it. I think you have a brain growing in your head. You are not what you look. You have nice, sweet eyes.

"Miss Lee," said Ruth. "I cannot find page seventeen because I can only read numbers to ten. Nobody showed me any more yet. Nobody showed me how to read many letters either. What should I do?"

Yes. That is the way it was. All throughout the school. I had a bunch of saplings on my hands, all so green and uprooted it would have scared a more trained person. The condition might have been fatal for us both had we not liked each other and both sides been willing to show some steady head.

Ignorance gives a sort of madness to a purposeful person. I stumbled and mumbled and bumbled among my children the greater part of that day, wondering what direction I would take with the next one if, O, God, we could survive this one. The trouble was, the kids saw no light in what they had already learned, and so there was no strength in it. I asked Idus to name the continents, and he did but could not say what a continent was. There was no understanding of what had been taken from the books. The trouble was, the words did not rap out any message to the brains. I saw the children sitting at their desks, prisoners. Quarantined. I heard my voice reading from the books, and it was all I could do to hold my own attention. The trouble was, there was no life in this kind of teaching.

At two o'clock, all of us waned-out, I declared school to be over for that day. The kids could not believe their good fortune. School was supposed to adjourn at three, not two. They thundered to the cloakroom for their wraps. Wrangles. *Hey, those are my rubbers, give 'em to me. Stop pushing. They ain't room in here for all of us. It was awful, worse'n L. C. I thought she'd be different, but she ain't. Shhhhh, she'll hear.*

The kids hurled themselves out both doors. Their cries of freedom filled the schoolyard, fading. I do not know what the people of the town thought to see their little folk scattering homeward, an hour early, swinging their lunch pails and boxes. Only Salem stayed behind. He said, "Why'd you let out early? You decided to quit already?"

"No. I have decided to do this job right. But first I have to decide how to decide where to start. I think one of the troubles in this school is nobody understands what it is he is reading."

"Reading ain't fun," said Salem. I thanked him for his help that day and told him to go on home, too. I hung around for a while waiting for the fire in the stove to die. Ruth Porter had left her lunch apple on my desk, and I went outside to divide it with Little Boy. I thought some of the parents might come to see the new schoolteacher. Nobody came.

The weather of the day had turned out better than I had foreseen. It had warmed a little, the sun spreading its brilliance across the hills. I had thought to spend that night with Merlie Bud and Dovie Luckabill, but on my way to their house changed my mind and went home instead. I thought the exercise would not hurt Little Boy.

CHAPTER EIGHT

O, those were the days. Bobo Birdwell brought us another letter from the Petifers saying Holtie's brother still lingered on the portal of death. The man who bought General Birdwell's store began to pay us regular visits, pressing us for what we owed him, and our cows strayed deep into the woods. In the cold, without enough clothing to keep them warm, Maw Maw and Paw Paw got out and scouted for the animals and did find them.

At night, under his quilt, Paw Paw coughed and I knew from the stealthy sound of it he was awake and restless.

He spent his days puttering around the half-erected new house, adjusting a log here, filling in a crack there. He made a kitchen work table, an eating table and six chairs.

The two old ones did not do any complaining to me about our conditions. I was getting madder and madder at Hutchens, Estie and Ora, who wrote postcards, not letters. Maw Maw said she thought they would come at Thanksgiving time.

I decided against Merlie Bud Luckabill's suggestion to stay any night with him and Dovie. I was always fearful of what I would or would not find at home, so on school days Little Boy and I went from Blue Ash Hollow to Pintail Fork each early morning, and late in the afternoons we returned. I was careful to feed my little burro double rations. Still, he grew lean.

The boy, Pup, from Copsey Springs showed up at school one day. He told me Sorrow and Winston Splitstone had taken over the raising of his little new brother. I said, "What do you mean?" He cast a grin and answered, "Mama gave him to Doc Sorrow and The Hermit to keep for a while. The Doc said to tell you hey."

I missed Sorrow and would lie awake at night making plans to go and visit her. I thought her relationship with The Hermit a little tacky, but I was glad she had it. There was never enough time to go and visit her, and she did not come. Estie sent Maw Maw a wool coat that her daughter, Florine, had outgrown.

When you think of man reaping as he has sowed you think usually along the lines of his having to pay finally. Oh-ho, the saddle has at last been put on the right horse.

How do you feel now, rascallion? It is not so nice and pleasant to feel the pinch of your misdeeds, is it, but you were warned a long time ago that justice would not forever be patient and blind.

Do you think man gets as he gives? I do not. Good parents frequently have bad children. That is the other side of the shield when speaking of man reaping as he has sowed.

The beginning of the job as schoolkeeper at Pintail Fork School was some huckleberry, owing to the fact the kids and I both were a little leery of how much the other knew. Dealing with the subject of volcanoes, the children and I had a confab like this:

"Miss Lee, you told me to write a paper about volcanoes, but I couldn't."

"Why not, Idus?"

"I couldn't. I don't unnerstand volcanoes."

"Idus, did you read your book?"

"Yes'm. I wondered if you did."

"I did when I was your age. Idus—"

"I don't mean to aggravate you, Miss Lee."

"You are not aggravating me, Idus. It is just that I have so much—all right, what do you not understand about volcanoes?"

"I don't unnerstand them. What are they?"

"A volcano is a mountain, Idus."

"Where?"

"Anywhere. A volcano can be anywhere."

"What's in it?"

"Fire."

"What causes the fire?"

"Oh, um, hot rocks."

"What makes 'em hot?"

"The fire, Idus, the fire."

"What starts the fire?"

"Oh, um, God."

"God?"

"Idus, it is simple. There are hot volcanoes just like there are cold rivers. The world is hot in some places."

"Is it gonna burn up?"

"It might someday."

"With us in it?"

"I reckon so. We have not got anywhere else to go. But let's not worry about—"

"Maybe we could all go to Africa. That's another continent, ain't it?"

"Sure."

"They got any volcanoes in Africa?"

Lord, are there volcanoes in Africa? Tell me quick. "Idus, we are not studying Africa. We are studying volcanoes. Now—"

"I just thought of somethin'. Wait a minute, I see somethin'. Africa's a different continent but it's still in the world."

"That is right. Of course it is."

"Then it wouldn't do us any good to go there, would it?"

"Idus, I did not say we should all pick up and move to Africa."

"You said God made the fire in volcanoes."

"Well, yes, I did say that. God made everything. That

is what I meant. Salem, go and open a window. It is too hot in here. And Idus, sit down and put your shoes on. Ruth, you go back to your seat. All of you go back to your seats. I am hearing sixth grade now."

"I think I should go home," said Ruth.

I said, "Ruth, you cannot go home now. I have not even heard your lessons yet. Go back to your seat."

"I am scared."

"Of what, for pity's sake?"

"Volcanoes. What if God was to decide to burn up the whole world about ten minutes from now?"

"Children, children, you should not get so excited. Sit down, all of you. Ruth—"

"You said it could happen. You said it might."

"Yes, but I did not mean any time soon. I meant hundred and hundreds of years from now."

"When we're all dead?"

"I guess so. Children—"

"I don't want to be dead. I'd be scared to be dead. I haven't seen but one dead person. He looked scared."

"Kids, there is not a thing to being dead. You will not even feel it. When you are dead you are resting, is all. What are you so scared of? The streets of heaven are paved with gold, and the angels are there, playing on their golden harps. Everything smells good, like flowers, and nobody is ever sick or goes hungry."

Whew. Whoever thought of putting volcanoes in geography books ought to have to answer to children about what being dead means too. Personally, I think when I am dead there will come a new creation of myself. In this land of unreal possibilities and come-thick shadows it is possible to have this notion. It comes to me strongest when the moon is full and white on the landscape and the stars of the Big Dipper and the Seven Sisters are lighted and the old barred owl, who lives in a tree on the other side of our creek calls, *hoo, hoo, hoo, hoo, hoo, hoo, hoo, aw*. There is something in the wild, unafraid darkness that renews the spirit. The old fellow in his moonlighted tree can laugh. He has reddish-brown eyes and a feathered muffler. As a child I made some queer studies.

Until Pup showed up one morning with a book of detective stories and another of tales of horror and terror, the children at Pintail Fork School and I had quite a bit of trouble with our reading sessions. We had to use the textbooks of William H. McGuffey, and if that man was alive today I think I could put some second thoughts in his head concerning what reading subjects will brace the minds of the young and what will leave them stupored.

Pup said his books had been given to him by The Hermit. I thought the stories in them were interesting enough, the detective ones being about desperadoes being outwitted in such places as Rattlesnake Gulch by sleuths who were themselves immune to bullets, and the horror tales about men who turned into beasts after swallowing mysterious potions and horsemen who galloped around the countryside, headless. I did not think there was anything amiss in the children enjoying these stories. They enlivened the school day and taught an interest in reading.

In a school like that one, the teacher is also expected to be janitor, but I thought this to be not a reasonable thing. The kids agreed with me, and all of us pitched in and cleaned the building and the yard. I gave the children a day's advance notice concerning this so we had plenty of rags, soap and brooms. Ruth Porter brought three pans of vanilla fudge, and after the job was done, we all sat down and ate it.

All of us were sorry to see Merlie Bud appear one morning, ready to take the job of teaching back. He paid me the amount we had agreed on, and I, thinking I was then without employment, lit out for home, but scarcely made it halfway before L. C., riding his little fawn-colored pony, caught up with me. He said Merlie Bud had no more got the kids settled to doing their lessons than he was taken sick again. I asked, "What is his trouble this time?" And L. C. answered, "He thinks he has the gout."

I said, "I am surprised to see you. I thought you were up in the north woods guiding hunting parties."

"A man has to get home once in a while to see his mother," said L. C.

After that I had what amounted to a full-time job, but the pay did not stretch to providing for three people. Paw Paw and I, he on one of his mules and I on Little Boy, went down to the store at Pioneer Gap one Saturday to buy supplies we needed, and the new owner refused to sell to us until we had paid him twelve dollars of what we owed him and he said each time we came we would have to do this. I did not blame this man. A debt is a debt.

The day after my school let out for the Thanksgiving holidays, a frigid rain drenched our area of the Ozarks and then a mass of cold air, moving down from the north, froze our ground and then a bunch of warm air moved up from the south and then we had a glaze storm. Every blade and tree, every post and length of fence, the field stubble, our barn and outbuildings all became coated with glittering, frozen water. The whole of our hollow gleamed like crystal glass, and when the wind moved through it we heard tinklings and crackings. The sun did not shine, and the birds did not fly.

We moved Maw Maw's chickens from the henhouse to the lower part of the barn and locked them and our animals in. It was cold enough so that we no longer needed to use the spring house in the creek to keep our milk and other dairy foods from spoiling. We put our pails of milk and pans of eggs, cream and butter on the shelves in the corner of the lower barn that Sorrow had used so many years as her laboratory. In the morning everything liquid was covered with a coating of ice.

Hutchens had written a postcard to say that he and Mispah would be coming to eat Thanksgiving dinner with us, and my grandparents, excited, brought a ham from Paw Paw's meathouse. It was full of skippers—little worms that have a liking for pork. They had worked their way through the ham; the meathouse was alive with them, we found. Over this tragedy Maw Maw came close to crying and Paw Paw put his lip in his teeth. When I looked at them, blue and pinched from the cold, bewildered by this latest trouble, with fear and defeat beginning to show in them, I hated Hutchens, Estie and Ora and I silently cussed them.

We could not eat the worm-infested meat. Paw Paw said we should dump all of it into the creek. He would not wait for the weather to clear; he would not wait for anything. In a fine, misty rain that turned immediately to ice when it hit the earth, we took all of the meat from the meathouse and carried it to the creek and threw it in. We stood together on the bank of the creek for a minute, feeling the sleet in our faces and looking at our hollow, glittering silver in the murky light. I thought Paw Paw's cough had worsened and doctored it that night with a tonic made from the fragrant leaves of the foal's foot plant.

Maw Maw said we would have stewed chicken with dumplings for our Thanksgiving dinner, and in the morning of the holiday killed two of her laying hens, which was a sacrifice. Had we had our dinner without company we would have eaten a jar of our preserved fish with a side dish of grits.

Hutchens and Mispah arrived early in the morning of the holiday, Hutchens heavier than I had ever seen him. Mispah wore a gold-colored wool dress with matching coat, black patent leather shoes and stockings so flimsy her legs appeared bare. Hutchens had thought to bring two bakery-bought mince pies in a white box tied with a string. Warmed by the fire from our stove, our quarters were roughly comfortable, probably recollective of the first Thanksgiving celebrated by the Pilgrims.

After a look around, Hutchens wanted to know where Sorrow was, and Paw Paw was quick to reply, "Oh, she had to go to one of her patients. I don't look for her back 'fore dark."

"I hope she has got some good horse legs under her," remarked Hutchens. "In all this ice the roads are dangerous." He admired the new table and chairs Paw Paw had built, and Maw Maw told him and Mispah about my school-keeping job.

I let Hutchens eat a generous dinner and then I got him to go down to the lower part of the barn with me. On the behalf of Maw Maw and Paw Paw, I thought the time had come for me to make an appeal to Hutchens. We stood in front of one of the cow stalls, and he did not help me with my end of the conversation. I said, "Hutchens, I hate to bring this up, but Maw Maw and Paw Paw have got to have some help to tide them through the winter. What I make and what Sorrow is able to give is not enough for all of us."

Hutchens never did have much of a conversation fund. . He said, "What, Littabelle? What's this?"

I said, "Hutchens, what you see up there now is not the way it is every day. You see only the best we have got because that is what Maw Maw and Paw Paw want you to see, but we are in a bad way. This barn is not suitable for Maw Maw and Paw Paw to live in. I could live under a tree and it would make no never-mind to me, but Maw Maw and Paw Paw feel the cold more than a person my age, and they go out and do the chores every day while Sorrow and I are away and we have to carry our water from the creek and Paw Paw does not get enough sleep any more. He gets up four or five times a night to stoke the fire. He is half-sick, I guess you noticed."

"I noticed him coughing a little," said Hutchens, sniffling his catarrh. "That kind of trouble runs in the Lee family. Paw Paw don't look any different to me than he ever has. Says he feels all right. When is Holtie Petifer coming back so you-call can finish the new house?"

"We do not know. Holtie's brother is on the brink of death, and I guess he and Ada are just going to wait it out in Louisiana. Hutchens, could you ask Maw Maw and Paw Paw to go back to town with you and stay? Just until the winter is over?"

"Oh," said Hutchens, drawing back a little. "I don't know about that. I just know they'd never agree to go. The house wasn't ever built big enough to hold two families, Littabelle. Mine and Mispah's is little; it just ain't big enough to hold four grown people."

You are empty-hearted, I thought, just like your sisters. I was strongly tempted to punch him in his well-fed face. I tried another tack. "The man who bought General Birdwell's store is hounding Paw Paw for what he owes him," I said. "I paid him a little on the account the last time we went down, but there is still a big amount due, and he will not sell us supplies unless we pay him some each time we go in."

Quickly Hutchens said, "I will send Paw Paw some money next week, and I will ask Ora and Estie to do the same. Don't look on us as monsters, Littabelle. You are just a kid, and livin' up here the way you always have with somebody to give you a roof over your head and put food in your mouth, you don't know what it is to have to get out and scratch for every dollar. Times is hard, a lot harder in town than they are up here."

We did not argue. My determination to succeed with

Hutchens in this instance might not have been strong enough. I think I was not graceful enough and spoiled my chances by jumping in with too much directness, but a person has to be true to the best he knows.

Hutchens walked around, idly looking at the chickens and animals; he observed that they seemed to be faring well enough, and presently we went back up the ladder to the loft. He and Mispah stayed for about another hour, but he did not discuss any finances with either Maw Maw or Paw Paw. Shortly after our visitors left, Paw Paw went to bed and I thought he might have the croup, though that is a sickness commonly suffered by children, not grown-ups.

I kept the fire going in the stove that night and the next morning did all the chores. It was another holiday from school, and I determined to go to Vulture Bluff to see Sorrow and The Hermit. I was not merely angry with Hutchens, I was *mad* with him and Estie and Ora too, and I thought the time had come to act with decision.

Before I went down the ladder, I cautioned Maw Maw to stay in, close to the fire. In his sleep Paw Paw coughed and was restive. His head felt feverish to my hand.

The glaze storm was over; the sun was out, and the ice was beginning to fall away from the trees and vegetation and our buildings. Little Boy and I went through the cold, quiet forest to Vulture Bluff, and we saw the birds coming from their places where they had sheltered during the storm. We traveled cautiously, for the floor of the woods was slick with melting ice.

Sorrow and Winston Splitstone acted glad to see me.

Mr. Splitstone had made the pup's little brother a cradle, and Sorrow had to display him to me. I said I thought he would do as far as looks were concerned. Sorrow seemed to have the notion that in some way he had become hers. He opened his eyes, saw me and screamed. Sorrow snatched him up and went to a rocker, crooning to the child.

Mr. Splitstone and I went outside and sat on his stoop. I said, "Well, I declare you do look better with your hair shorter. Did Sorrow cut it for you?"

"Yes," replied The Hermit.

"Does the child have a name yet?" I asked.

"No," said The Hermit.

"That is strange," I said. "If the child's mother is not going to give him one and you and Sorrow are going to raise him, I see it as your duty to give him one."

"Sorrow was thinking about naming him either Will or Jackson," said The Hermit. "She and I are going to get married next week."

We sat gazing at each other. After a while I said, "In that case you can help me out."

"No," said The Hermit, "I can't either. I am about as broke as they come, Missy, and am being forced to thinking about taking up a vocation."

"I didn't mean I wanted you to help me out with money."

"Oh? How then?"

"I need somebody to help me think what I can do about Hutchens, Ora and Estie. They act like Maw Maw and Paw Paw are not even their parents. They will not send even a dollar to help out. For myself, I do not care, but for Maw Maw and Paw Paw I think it is criminal, what they are suffering."

"Yes," agreed The Hermit. "Maybe there ought to be a law against kids treatin' their parents the way your Maw Maw and Paw Paw are being treated." He rubbed the air with his fingers and, like a schoolboy, twisted his feet back and forth.

After a while I said, "Maybe there is one."

The Hermit regarded me. With a deepening frown he said, "No."

"How do you know? You don't know everything. I am just saying, what if there is one? Could I make it work for me? For Maw Maw and Paw Paw?"

"Littabelle—"

"All right, it is crazy. Everything is crazy. But what if I could? How would I find out? Where would I start?"

"Hoooeee," murmured The Hermit. "You'd have to start with a lawyer, I think. But Littabelle—"

"I do not know any lawyer. Do you?"

"No. The only time I ever went to court with anything was back east when I was young and I acted as my own."

"Can you do that?"

"I did. Littabelle—"

"Mr. Splitstone, I have got to have some help from somewhere. Just to get us through the winter. You and Sorrow cannot give me any, that is plain enough. I am going to get some help from somebody. Now then. Do you know any lawyer?"

"You're crazy," said The Hermit.

"Yes. Do you know any lawyer?"

"I heard tell of a judge at Pioneer Gap. Don't know him personally, but I've heard of him." Oh, The Hermit was unwilling, but he was staring at me, as if he saw in me some exciting, pleasing secret.

I said, "Is this judge a lawyer? You said I would need to start with a lawyer, so why are you telling me about a judge?"

"A judge is better than a lawyer," informed The Hermit. "This one is. He is Judge Levoy Marriage."

"That is a queer name for a judge," I said.

"He fits his name," said The Hermit, and then he would not talk to me any more.

CHAPTER NINE

Paw Paw's croup turned out to be a bad case of the grippe, and I ministered to him with one medicine made from the roots of a little plant known as bird-on-the-wing and another made from the tops and leaves of the perennial herb, agueweed. For two weeks he was confined to his bed, refusing to take anything but hot, buttered grits, broth and herb tea for nourishment. I told him I thought he would dry up and melt away to nothing, and he grinned feebly and said, "Just you tend to your own knittin' and let me tend to mine. Tomorrow I'm a-gonna git up outa this bed and show you and Maw

Maw the old man ain't done for yet."

The tomorrows came and went, and he did not leave his bed for any length of time worth mentioning. I thought he might die in it, and during the time I had to be away from home worried about him and Maw Maw and the state of our affairs. Hutchens sent three dollars. Nothing came from Estie or Ora. I kept shying away from starting any action against them.

One morning, going down the ladder, I felt sick and dizzy myself and paused midway for a minute, waiting for the feelings to pass. Probably something you did not eat, I thought. The little illness went away, and I finished descending and went on outside and whistled for Little Boy.

It was then December, and the hours of darkness were lengthening by a minute or so each day. We were ahead of the calendar in our winter; it was at hand, with frozen ground and flurries of fine snow and the gray forest mists like cold, floating ghosts. Winter in our part of the Ozarks is a time for calling up the heart's fortitude.

By lantern light Little Boy breakfasted while I milked the cows, and the chickens in their nests watched me, cocking their heads the way chickens do. Maw Maw's rooster hopped down from his perch and strutted, and I said to all of the fowl, "You had better enjoy life while you can. Spring is a long time away. We might have to eat you before then. What we get from these cows will keep us alive maybe, but it doesn't stick to the ribs much." I set the pails of warm milk on the shelves in Sorrow's laboratory. The lantern was needed at home so I extinguished its flame and left it at the entranceway of the barn for Maw Maw to find. She and Paw Paw still slept.

There was no moon. It was still an hour to daylight when Little Boy and I set out for Pintail Fork. In spite of its fleece lining, Holtie's surtout was not as warm as I could have wished it to be, and I coaxed Little Boy to run to warm us both. We found our trail and slowed to a walk. I put my hands in my sleeves and pulled my hair down over my ears. Life in the region was quiet.

Halfway to Pintail Fork I knew I was sick. I told Little Boy to stop and I dismounted and sat on the ground beside a clump of winterbloom, still with some of its yellow flowers clinging to its dry, shriveled stems. They looked out of place in the graying light. I had a headache, a bad one, and was nauseous. My bones had started to hurt. Lord God, I thought, I am sick but I cannot be sick. I have got two old, helpless people depending on me. Get up and go, girl.

I made it to school but spent the day in the cloakroom, lying on a pallet made of my coat. Salem conducted the classes and every once in a while crept in to squat beside me. "How you feelin'?"

"Terrible. Do you have to twitch and wiggle like that?"

"You should go to Mister Merlie Bud's house."

"No. I'll be all right pretty soon. What are the children doing? I cannot hear them."

"They're bein' quiet 'cause they know you're sick. We've been talking about bees. Idus wants to build the hives tomorrow. I told him you said we had to wait till spring. Ain't that what you said?"

"Yes. We'll start our colonies in the spring."

"Didn't you say we could sell the honey?"

"I was always able to sell mine."

"What if you ain't our teacher come spring?"

"I'll come anyway and help you with the bees."

"It's snowin'."

"That's good."

"It's been snowin' all day. You better spend the night with Mister Merlie Bud and Miss Dovie."

"No. I'll go home. My grandfather has the grippe, and I cannot be away from home any longer than I have to be."

"L. C. was here at noon."

"What do you mean? It is not noon yet. Is it? What time is it?"

"Most three o'clock," said Salem. "You've been asleep."

"What did L. C. want?"

"Nothing. Said for me to tell you he'd teach school tomorrow if you was too sick to come. Said to tell you he wouldn't tell Mister Merlie Bud, so you wouldn't lose any money. For friendship, he said. L. C. likes you. You like him?"

"Yes, he is all right. As men go, that is."

"You don't like men?"

"I guess I can tolerate them. I like my grandfather. I have got an uncle I wouldn't let slop my hogs even if they were starving to death."

"L. C. said you was gutty. One time he had another girl. I didn't like her so one day he told her to go away and not bother us any more. I came in here to get the coats and stuff. It's time for everybody to go home."

I got up and went out into the classroom and stood at the window, watching the children run from the schoolyard. The snow was coming down thick and fast. Earlier in the day the wind had made scudded drifts of it in the narrow road running past the school. There were no tracks in it; it was smooth and blue-shaded. The wind had moved out to the open hills.

Salem had come to stand beside me. He pulled the ends of his hair, played with the tip of his nose and his earlobes. I said, "Salem, what is wrong with you that you cannot be still, even for one minute?"

He said, "Miss Lee, I think a witch might've spelled and fitified me when I was a little kid. If you and me is the friends I think we are, you will just have to put up with it. L. C. took Little Boy home with him so he wouldn't have to stand out in the snow all day. Want me to go git him for you? You still going back to Blue Ash Hollow today? If you are, L. C. and me'll go part way with you. You wait here and I'll go get L. C. and Little Boy."

Inside Holtie's coat, I sat at the teacher's desk and waited for them. The snow had begun to stick to the windows; there were big, fat blooms of it on the outside sills. I wondered how deep it would be in the woods between Pintail Fork and Blue Ash Hollow. I knew I had the grippe, and I wondered how bad it would get before it would better. I wondered how long I could hold out against it and I thought, If something should happen to me, what will happen to Maw Maw and Paw Paw? I thought about the man named Judge Levoy Marriage in Pioneer Gap.

When L. C. and Salem came back with Little Boy, I went outside and stood with them for a minute in the falling snow. L. C. said, "Littabelle, you had better not try to go home in this. You're sick. Haven't you got enough sense to know that?"

"I thank you for taking care of Little Boy for me," I said. "Help me mount. I am going home. Did you say you would take the school for me tomorrow?"

"You are crazy," said L. C. "You are too gutty for a girl. A man don't like to look at a girl who is so gutty."

"You are free to look the other way any time you get ready," I said.

L. C. helped me up on Little Boy's back. "Want Salem and me to go part way with you?"

"No. I am feeling all right except for a little headache. If you are serious about keeping the school for me tomorrow, I thank you. I will be back the day after."

"I will keep it for you," said L. C. "People have been known to get lost in the woods in snow storms. Don't get off your trail and don't stop to rest. You can rest when you get home. People have been known to die while restin' in a snowbank. It makes them drowsy, and they go to sleep and never wake up."

"You talk like an old woman," I said. I nudged Little Boy's flank with my foot, and we moved out. Several times during the home-going journey we stopped and I got down and ate a handful of snow. Against the bases of the black-topped trees it lay in shining, drifted lines. The falling flakes felt good in my face though not, I am sure, in Little Boy's.

There was another crisis waiting for me. When Little Boy and I got to Blue Ash Hollow and rode into our yard, I saw Maw Maw standing near the bank of our creek. Her head was bare, there was snow in her hair, and I saw that her skirt was wet and that she had on only one shoe. I got down and called out to her. "Maw Maw, you should not be out here! It's freezing! Why are you only wearing one shoe? Are you looking for something?"

She came toward me and I saw how despaired she was. "Oh, Littabelle, our cows have strayed again. I've been looking everywhere for them, clear back in the woods, everywhere. But I can't find them, and I lost my shoe. I don't know where. I didn't even feel it come off. I just looked down and it was gone. Oh, Littabelle—"

"Go to the loft, Maw Maw."

"I have to find my shoe, Littabelle. And we will have to find the cows. Where could they be? I've looked on this side of the creek and the other."

I said, "Maw Maw, you have got to get out of this weather. Do you want pneumonia? I will find your shoe and I will find the cows if they are to be found. Put Little Boy in the barn for me, will you?"

"Yes," said Maw Maw. "Yes." She took Little Boy's reins in her hand, and they went to the barn together, and I spent a few minutes looking in the snow for the lost shoe but could not find it and then I went across the foot-bridge and into the woods again, calling, "So boss! So boss!" The snow shrieked under my feet and dusk came on. Some of the trees had small icicles dripping from their branches, and I broke one off and sucked on it and I heard the barred owl laughing, *hoo, hoo, hoo, hoo, hoo, hoo, hoo, aw.*

Presently I brushed the snow from an old stump and sat on it and said to myself, "Well, Missy, the cows are gone and they might not ever come back. Maybe they are tired of Arkansas and have gone to Missouri; who can say? And Maw Maw's shoe is gone and might not be found till next spring. And I am sick. This is some predicament, some predicament. Sorrow said she thought the world was trying to get rid of her; I think it is trying to get rid of Paw Paw, Maw Maw and me."

The snow was coming down faster, and the wind was picking up. I thought I could hear the rush of Rumpus River, and I pictured it, tumbling in its wild, cold trough. I pictured what I would look like, sitting frozen to death on the stump. My headache was immense, and I felt a dangerous languor steal over me. Maw Maw has only one shoe, I thought, and I wept and continued to sit there, letting my lap fill up with snow.

Well, people do not die sitting on stumps in the woods just because they might have a passing wish for it. There comes a moment, when you have gone down as far as you can, when you have to start back up. That is the life in you getting mad. When I was mad enough I stood up, dusted the snow from myself, and went home. Maw Maw had got out the only other pair of shoes she owned, ones discarded months before. We cut new inner soles for them from a pasteboard box. "They will do for a while," said

Maw Maw. "Paper is warm."

"They will not stand up to getting wet," I said. "The cows will come back when they get hungry enough. I will look for them again tomorrow evening when I get home."

Paw Paw came from his bed to eat supper with Maw Maw and me, and I had to admit to him that I might be coming down with a slight cold. After my meal, which I had no taste for, I gave Paw Paw half a dozen dried, sweetbrier hips and chewed a dozen myself. Great dosages of these are good in a fight with grippe.

The next morning I told myself I felt well enough to tackle a meeting with Judge Levoy Marriage, if I could arrange one; instead of going to Pintail Fork, I went to Pioneer Gap. I stopped first at General Birdwell's store, and the new owner there told me Judge Marriage lived in a stone house in back of the First Church of God. "But you won't get the judge outa bed at this hour unless it's a matter of life and death."

"That is what it might be," I said.

Preparing to do a day's business, the store owner was rushing around tidying the place. He wanted to know if I had had prior dealings with the judge and when I said no, he said, "Well, he's a queer one. Don't tell him I said so but he is."

I asked, "How is he queer?" And the store owner replied, "People say he don't stick to the laws when he hands down his judgments. He makes them up to suit hisself and you can like it or lump it. You didn't happen to bring me any money on account, did you?"

I answered, "No, but if I am successful in what I am going to see Judge Marriage about, we will be able to pay the whole debt off very soon." The store owner did not offer me a cup of his coffee though a potful steamed on the back of his stove.

Pioneer Gap lay under a snowfall that might have been two feet deep in places. The sun was on the hills of the town though, and the temperature was rising. Little Boy is a good snow traveler and did not flounder going through the drifts to Judge Marriage's house.

My first thought of this man was a jarring one: Something has sucked all of his blood out and he has turned to cardboard, I thought. Except for his eyes. His eyes drowsed behind their lids, yet they perceived everything, and what they had perceived in another time might have turned him the way he was. He was old and papery and sick-humored and had an ill welcome for me, yet when I persisted in telling him of my mission and he began to listen, an old, dying bonfire in him was kindled. My predicament seemed to strengthen him. You might have thought I had invented it for the sole purpose of bringing it to him to solve, the way he took hold of it. His voice whistled through his teeth. "You say this aunt of yours, the one living at Vulture Bluff now, is daffy?"

I said, "No, I did not say she was daffy. I said she suffered a little insult to her head and now she is strange. She has married a man named Mr. Winston Splitstone, and they have taken a baby, belonging to a woman at Copsey Springs, to raise. I was midwife to this woman at the time this child was born. He is fat and sassy now."

"You are a midwife?"

"I am a yarb doctor when I am not a schoolkeeper, sir."

"Is that a fact."

"Yes, sir."

"Are you a good yarb doctor?"

"I do not think so, sir. When I was younger, I never thought the day would come when I would have to meet my whys and wherefores and so I did a lot of piddling and faddling. I wasted a lot of time that I have got to make up for now. I am not a lazy woman. Not one to sit at home stitching pretties, waiting for some man to bring home bacon to me. I can earn my own bacon and enough for my grandparents too, but I have got to be allowed a fair start. That is why I am here. I thought you could help me get one."

"My mother was a yarb doctor," said Judge Marriage.

"Yes, sir."

"I never heard of any law that compels children to care for their aged parents."

"You mean there isn't one? But that is not right. When we first started this talk you said there was a law that made parents care for their children. Now why is there not a law to cover the ground in the other direction?"

"Calm your excitement," said Judge Marriage. "I cannot think and listen to your babbling at the same time."

"Your pardon, Judge. It's only that I—"

"Are you sick?"

"A little. But never mind that. What about all these

books? Would not one of them tell you if there is a law such as the kind I am talking about?"

"I will do a little research on that," answered the judge. "But mainly when I hear a case, I don't depend on any book to tell me what to do. Those pettifoggers in Little Rock don't know the problems of you hill people so make no provision for them. I tell you what. I will give you the name of a lawyer to go and see. You tell him what you've told me. Then we'll see."

"What lawyer? What do I need another lawyer for? Aren't you one?"

"I am a circuit judge, young lady."

"I don't know what that is."

"A circuit judge is a man like myself, learned in the law, who goes around the state hearing court cases. You will have to have a lawyer plead your case for you. I will sit on the bench and judge it. When the time comes."

"Judge, sir. I do not have any money to hire any lawyer."

The judge fell silent. I considered my position and after a minute or two said, "I will be my own lawyer. I will get up in your court and plead my own case. When could you judge it?"

"Young lady, you don't know what you're saying."

"Yes, I do."

"Your uncle Hutchens and your aunts Ora and Estie would have to be subpoenaed."

"What does that mean?"

"You see?"

"Well, tell me. Help me. I tell you once again, Judge,

I am desperate, and somebody has just blamed-sure got to help me."

"A subpoena," said Judge Marriage, "is a judicial writ requiring a person to appear at a specified time and place under penalty for default."

"I see."

"There would need to be three issued. Child, you can't handle this."

"I can handle it. How do I go about making those subpoenas? What do I say in them?"

"They're special pieces of paper. Child—"

"Do you have any? Could I borrow three?"

Eventually that man wrote out the three subpoenas himself, fixing on them the date he would hear my case against Hutchens, Ora and Estie, and though it was irregular, he said it was, he guaranteed they would be hand-delivered. He said the whole proceeding was irregular. By the time we got through with it, he was a little vexed, I thought. I thanked him, and he said, "Rats."

CHAPTER TEN

After my meeting with Judge Marriage, I went home and gave Maw Maw a lie-excuse about my being there earlier than I should have been. I told her it was a half-holiday at my school. Paw Paw's head was still dry and feverish to my touch. I thought there was a good chance of his grippe turning into something more lasting and serious.

I thought we could both get over the "bugs" that sapped at our strength if I could lay my hands on some good, red meat. Now each time I went from the loft to the lower half of the barn I thought the chickens watched me fearfully; I thought they must surely hate the terrified squawks each time we had to slaughter another of their number. There is no merciful way to kill a chicken. Fish are smarter. It seemed to me those in our creek had thought up more ways to elude my pole and hook than was right. They hid themselves in the rocks and, except for an occasional goggle-eye, ignored my bait. One evening when I went to the loft with just one scrawny one for our skillet, I said to Maw Maw we should butcher another of our hogs. She backed off from the suggestion saying, "We can't. The sow'll farrow in another sixty or seventy days and that'll be a fresh start for us. The boar Paw Paw wouldn't part with, not for anything. Don't fret him now with how we're going to make out. We'll get by some way."

To get by some way, that is the pattern of the old.

It aggravated and disgusted me that I did not know more about the treatment for illnesses affecting the throat and chest. In their bottles and boxes, on their shelves, Sorrow's array of medicaments was more than a bit of a riddle. Looking at them, trying to remember which Sorrow had told me was used for what, I thought—Missy, you might as well be growing dogtail cotton in your head for all the good your brain has done you. You should know about these things; you were raised with them. And you should know what makes a volcano and not have to blame the fires in them on God. And you should know it was the Spaniard, Balboa, who was the first one to clap his eyes on the Pacific Ocean, not Christopher Columbus. A little kid had to bring that mistake to your attention. You had better be giving your whys and wherefores a second thought or two. If he has not already, one of these days one of the children at Pintail Fork School will go home and tell his daddy you did not know the difference between an island and a peninsula and then the devil will have you by your coattails. You will be out of a job.

The temperature in our quarters probably hung somewhere around sixty degrees as long as we kept the fire roaring in the stove. The dung smell, rising to us from the barn floor, was strong. The weather did not break.

The day after my meeting with Judge Marriage, I went direct from school to The Hermit's place at Vulture Bluff, thinking I could get Sorrow to come and have a look at Paw Paw and at the same time look for our cows. I had Holtie Petifer's carbine with me and extra loadings for it.

Between Blue Ash Hollow and Vulture Bluff our hinterland lay in deepest cold. The trees on the snowscape were dark and still. I thought I saw a red wolf lurking in a cedar brake, and I held my carbine ready and gave a wide berth to that area. Keeping a keen lookout for the cows, I called, "So boss! So boss!" The birds and small animals of the forest were lost in a sort of hibernation. The thought came to me that our cows might be lying dead beneath the snowdrifts or had wandered as far as Rumpus River and fallen into its dangerous current and drowned, or been attacked by a pack of wolves and killed.

Without spotting a sign of the cows, I reached The Hermit's place at Vulture Bluff. There was smoke coming from its chimney, but no one appeared to answer my door banging. I went around to the back of the place and looked through the window and saw Sorrow sitting in a rocking chair. She was holding the infant belonging to the woman at Copsey Springs. He looked to me as if he had gained ten pounds. I shouted, "Aunt Sorrow, you deaf? Did you not hear me banging on the front door? Let me in!"

"The door's open!" she shouted back. "Aw, you woke up the baby."

It took half an hour to quiet the child. He would not let me hold him. Every time I smiled at him or tried to stroke his little bald head, he would shriek and kick. "You're scarin' him," said Sorrow. "He don't like the way you look. Look in the cupboard and see is there not a rind of bacon. There should be one left over from our breakfast this morning. That'll quieten him down."

Surprised, I said, "Aunt Sorrow, should you not be feeding this baby milk?"

"He swigs it like a calf," said Sorrow, grinning. "But in between times, he likes to suck on bacon rind. Gimme that big hunk there." Sure enough the rind quieted the baby, and Sorrow took him to another room where he went to sleep. Sorrow then came back to the kitchen and told me Mr. Splitstone had gone to Pioneer Gap to see about getting some kind of work and that the boy, Pup, was about somewhere.

I asked, "Are you married yet?"

"Yes," replied Sorrow, sitting in her rocker. "How're Paw Paw and Maw Maw?"

"Paw Paw has the grippe," I answered and waited,

thinking she would offer to go home with me.

After a time she said, "I'll not go home with you to see about Paw Paw, Littabelle. If I did, I'd never make it back here, and this is where I want to be. This is where I'm going to be. All my life I've run to see about Paw Paw and Maw Maw, and they don't think a whit more of me for doing it than they do Hutchens and Ora and Estie. Am I right or am I wrong?"

"I think you are right," I said.

"I have named the baby Ward."

"That is a happy name for a child."

"For the grippe I always use velvet dock leaves. Boil a handful in a little water and get Paw Paw to breathe the steam. Make him some tea from the leaves and get him to drink it. Keep him warm and feed him as good as you can. A medical doctor could tell you more and better what to do, but that's all I know to tell you. Don't hold it against me I won't go home with you now, Littabelle."

"I don't."

"I'm going to stay here. I should have come here twenty years ago. It is wrong of a son or daughter to give up his life for his parents. He's only got one to live in this world, same as they. Am I right or am I wrong?"

"I think you are right," I said.

"You had better be thinking about that," warned Sorrow. "If I was your age again, I'd fly outa these hills 'fore sunup tomorrow morning. If I had to crawl, I'd crawl, but I'd get out. If I was you, I'd be thinkin' about making somethin' outa myself. You'll never do it here 'cause there's nobody smart enough here to teach you. Are the

Petifers back yet?"

"No," I replied. "I had better be going."

Sorrow made no move to rise and go to the door with me. She is finished with us, I thought. And I thought— Well, I do not blame her. All those years of doing for Maw Maw and Paw Paw. It is true; they do not think any more of her for doing it than they do of Hutchens, Ora and Estie.

In the yard I stood for a minute beside Little Boy, feeding him some corn from my coat pocket. The late light of the afternoon lay on the smooth drifts surrounding The Hermit's quiet cabin. Smoke rose from its chimney, and a touch of winter sun sparkled its windows. Velvet dock leaves for pneumonia, I thought. And I thought: Sorrow could have been somebody, a real doctor, if she had had half a chance. She should have done something about Hutchens, Ora and Estie a long time ago. They are going to help me with Maw Maw and Paw Paw even if I have to jerk knots in them. Even if I have to drag them to the United States Capital and bang on the President's door.

In the woods again only a little way, I met Pup, who appeared in the path before me with his arms upraised. I thought he had been larking, but he said no, he had been working. "I'm keepin' a eye on Mr. Splitstone's whiskey still while he's gone. Him and me started a new batch the other day. You want to look? It's just down that little hill yonder."

I said, "No, I do not want to see any whiskey still. If you are not careful, Mr. Splitstone will make an outlaw of you."

Pup rubbed his cold-red ears. "I saw a deer just now. If I had a gun, I would've killed it, but all I've got is this here knife."

I got down and stood beside Pup. "Where did you see a deer?"

Pup pointed. "Through there. Back in them trees. You ever killed one?"

"No."

"Me either. I bet it'd be fun."

"Pup," I said, "it is wrong to kill anything for fun. For food, that is different."

"Let's go get that deer," said Pup, and took Little Boy's reins from my hand and tied them to an evergreen. He did that as if we were related, and we started off down the slope in front of us as if we had suddenly become that way. Clannish and staunch together. We did not speak. Pup put his hand on my arm and patted it. The shadows of the trees lay black on the snow sheen, and the breath from our mouths was faintly blue. We went down the slope, the snow crunching beneath our feet, sinking sometimes in places where it had not hardened, and we saw the tracks of the deer. We went on several more paces before we saw the animal standing alone in a deer trail. It was a buck with antlers and a white, powderpuff tail. Pup's hand, closing around my arm, commanded me. We stopped, and the animal lifted his head; we observed each other. I could not gauge the distance between us. He was without fear. He stood motionless, watching.

Pup whispered to me, "Don't move quick. Bring your gun up slow."

There was the distance between us, and there were the blue-shadowed snow dunes. I could not have seen the animal's clear, beautiful eyes, yet I saw them. And I thought I saw in them what all of nature should be to human beings—a glimpse of God.

In other times I had killed for food and the experience had not been bad. I had not been squeamish about it, yet this time I could not, could not. Something inside me unfolded, rushing, illuminating. Stunned by this feeling I could not understand, I could not move. I felt ugly and naked.

Pup whispered urgently, "Bring your gun up slow."

I brought the gun up slow. It was heavy, heavier than in reality it was. I lowered it.

Pup's eyes were ablaze. He whispered urgently. "What's wrong?"

"Nothing."

"You sick?"

"No."

"Why you cryin'?"

"I'm not."

"Aren't you gonna kill him? Don't you want him?"

"No."

"But he's right there! It'd only take one shot! One!"

"No. I would rather die."

"Gimme the gun then, I'll do it."

"No. Get away from me. You want a slap? I'll give you one. Back off."

Mad, Pup backed off. The clouds were going across the frosty sky, and we two humans and the wild, beautiful animal continued to stand there, watching each other. I thought—He has used all of his powers to stay alive. You have no right, no right.

Away down the deer trail there was a movement of some kind and the deer, alerted, turned and bounded off, his hooves sending up little floes of snow.

Pup and I went back up the slope to the spot where we had left Little Boy. Pup was very much irked and put out with me. He said, "You had him dead to rights. You could have had him with one shot, just one."

How could I tell him what I felt? It was not just the deer to be explained. It was the flashing, tumbling shift I had felt inside myself while standing with my gun raised and pointed at the animal. He had brought me to some kind of a crossroad in my existence. It was an arrival, adding in some way, pointing in some way, to the meaning of my life. The deer was an ingredient of our land, and so he was an ingredient of myself. To be on the side of life where the Lord had placed me and to know it the way He intended me to know it, that is what the deer had shown me. But I could not tell Pup these things. So I said, "Pup, I could not kill that deer. He trusted me too much."

"You're a sissy girl."

"He has been out here in the woods a long time and he loves being here as much as we do. Don't you see?"

"You talk crazy," said Pup and kicked at the snow. After a moment he said, "He was sure pretty. Want me to give you a boot-up?"

Going home I looked for our cows again but did not see hide nor hair of them. I told Maw Maw Sorrow would come to have a look at Paw Paw as soon as she could. I was getting pretty good at telling these little cover-up lies.

I found the velvet dock leaves in one of Sorrow's medicine jars and doctored Paw Paw according to her prescription. I also drank some of the tea made from them and I thought it helped us both.

That night, just before our bedtime, the Petifers came. Holtie's brother was finally dead. Ada had brought us a pot of beef and vegetable stew, and Paw Paw wrapped his quilt around him and came from his bed to sit at the table and eat a bowl of it. I thought—He is better. It was only the grippe and lack of touch with humans. Ada and Holtie made Paw Paw and Maw Maw smile when they told of some of their experiences in Louisiana.

Later on in that night I heard my old barred owl, laughing in his snowy tree. *Hoo, hoo, hoo, hoo, hoo, hoo, hoo, aw.*

CHAPTER ELEVEN

Discontent is what makes people change, and maybe this is a better part of life. There is a kind of this that works for our betterment, making us pause to look back on the narrow, squandered roads we may have traveled and then forward to the more open, wider ones, lying just around the next bend, beyond the next hill.

The day after the Petifers got back from Louisiana, Bobo Birdwell came riding up the snow-packed road on his mule to bring me a notice from Judge Levoy Marriage, confirming the date he would hear my case against Hutchens, Ora and Estie. Three days hence I would, according to his order, appear in his court in Pioneer Gap at nine o'clock in the morning.

It was late in the day, and I felt sorry for Bobo, sitting on his mule in the snow. He had not waited to deliver the letter to me on our regular mail day but had made a special trip because the envelope looked "official."

I felt like I owed him at least a partial confidence. "It is about some business I have in Pioneer Gap this coming Friday. How is the road between here and there?"

"Terrible," answered Bobo, blowing his breath into his gloved hands.

"Do you think a car could come up on it?"

"No. You'd have to be bent on killin' yourself to try it. The county has got it closed off. If you're thinkin' of taking care of any business in Pioneer Gap come Friday, you'd best ride your grandpa's mule down. Your burro might have a hard time gettin' you there."

"If you could spare the time, I could give you a hot drink," I said.

"I cannot spare the time," said Bobo. I stood there, waiting for him to go but he made no move in that direction so I said, "If you can keep a secret, I will tell you what my business with Judge Marriage is. I am bringing warrants against some people. He is going to hear the case on Friday."

"Great day in the mornin'," said Bobo.

"I have not told anybody else, Bobo."

"No? Well, I'm jiggered. I won't tell anybody, of course. Not if you don't want me to. You've been tellin' me your secrets all your life, and I never tattled on you yet."

"This one is different. It is serious. I am bringing warrants against Hutchens, Ora and Estie for parent-neglect."

"Lord have mercy!" exclaimed Bobo. "I never heard of such a thing. Parent-neglect. Well, that's rich. Who's your lawyer?"

"I do not have one. I am going to be my own."

Bobo stroked his chin and stared down at me. His old face laughed and it was a gay and eager sound.

I said, "Bobo, it is not funny."

"No," agreed Bobo, straightening his face. "It ain't. It's rich though. Do your grandfolks know about this, Littabelle?"

"No. I will tell them after it is done. Anybody can be a lawyer, Bobo. All you have to do is get a judge to say he will hear your case and then get up and tell the truth about it. Listen, Bobo, I want you to do me a favor. If any letters come for Maw Maw and Paw Paw, could you just hold them? Not deliver them?"

Bobo was turning his mule around. "No, I couldn't do that, Littabelle. It would be against the rules of my job. But since today wasn't my regular day to come here and I came anyway to bring you your letter from Judge Marriage, I won't be comin' again 'fore Saturday. You worried one of your aunts or your uncle might write a letter to your grandfolks tellin' them about your plans? I don't know why. Even if that happened, they wouldn't know what the letters said till you got home from your job. Unless, since you got to be a schoolkeeper, you've taught 'em how to read."

"No," I said, "I haven't had the time for that, but the

· 136 ·

Petifers are back. They can read."

"Yeah," said Bobo. "I stopped at their place on the way up. Ada's cousin ain't the friendliest person in the world, is she?"

I said, "Oh, I think she just likes to be left alone. Ada said she was going back home in a couple of days."

"That road out there is bad," commented Bobo. "I durned near broke my fool neck on it while ago. I don't know why I keep on with this job. Anybody else standin' in my shoes would retire. I'm old enough. 'Cept who could they get to take over this work if I quit?"

"Do not look at me when you ask that question," I said. "I am laying out other plans for myself."

The discontent was in me, and the way it was deepening and heightening was a little alarming. My children at the Pintail Fork School accused me of the change. Said Idus, "When you first come here to keep us, you weren't so finicky. How come you got so finicky all of a sudden?"

"Because I want to be better than I was," I answered. "And smarter."

"Why?"

"Because I am tired of being the way I was. I don't want to be myself any more. I want to be somebody else."

"Why?"

"Because I don't want to be like some other people I have known."

"Is that why you're readin' all those books you got from Mr. Merlie Bud?"

"Of course."

"I never saw so many books," said Idus. "He must've been savin' them for a hundred years. I'll bet he never did read them all."

"That is his business," I said. "Let us get back to the lesson, Idus. Now tell me. What is eight times eight?"

"I dunno. Miss Lee, when you first come here you said it was God put the fires in volcanoes. Now you say they're from gas in the ground poppin' off."

"You had better be glad I am smarter than I was then and have the bravery to admit my mistakes," I said. "What is eight times eight?"

"I dunno."

"What do you mean, you don't know?"

"I mean I dunno. That's what I mean. I dunno. I dunno."

"IDUS, YOU HAVE GOT TO KNOW! THAT IS WHAT YOU ARE HERE FOR! TO KNOW! TO LEARN! THAT IS WHAT I AM HERE FOR! TO TEACH! WHAT IS EIGHT TIMES EIGHT?"

"Thirty-six."

"IT IS NOT!"

"What is it then?"

"EIGHT TIMES EIGHT IS SIXTY-FOUR! SIXTY-FOUR! HOW CAN YOU THINK THE ANSWER IS THIRTY-SIX WHEN IT IS SIXTY-FOUR! EIGHT TIMES EIGHT IS SIXTY-FOUR, IDUS!"

"Miss Lee, you are killin' my ears. I think I am going deaf. All right, all right, eight times eight is sixty-four. Sixty-four. Sixty-four. I got it now. You see if I haven't. You ask me again tomorrow and I'll tell you eight times eight is sixty-four. Can we talk about beekeeping now?"

The children and I wrote to the county agent asking

for books on the subject of beekeeping, and while we waited for them to come, made plans to set up an apiary in the far corner of the school yard. This spot would be shaded by trees in warm and hot weather and there would be good air drainage. A cold, shallow stream in the valley below the school would provide fresh, good water. The corn, clover and fruit plants of the hillside farms would be a good source of nectar and pollen. We made black-board sketches of the hives we would build as soon as the weather warmed enough for outdoor working.

Royce Fredericks had lost his appetite for chalk. He was my little artist, spending his recess time decorating the top of our blackboard with drawings of red-berried holly. L. C. Luckabill came with some Christmas Victrola records, and I asked him if he would be deputy for me on the day I would have my hearing before Judge Marriage at Pioneer Gap. He consented.

The day came, and on Paw Paw's mule I left home before daybreak. The snow on the road between Blue Ash Hollow and Pioneer Gap was not so deep as Bobo Bird-well had led me to believe. Mules are steady animals and not high-strung. We went past the Petifers' place, which was still dark, and I thought I heard a coyote howling from one of the empty corn fields in back of it. I thought of our lost cows and I thought of the job that lay ahead.

Some people think of winter as being the dead season. It is not true. Sometime when it is winter and there is snow on the ground, stop beside a tree and have a look at its frozen buds. Winter has not destroyed them. They are there, in their shells, ready to burst come the first spring warmth. You might see a pileated woodpecker, flashing red, white and black among the evergreens. Tracks in the snow tell their own story.

The mule and I continued down the road toward Pioneer Gap, and the day came, clear and lighted with sun. I had had no breakfast and felt light-headed. The mule and I went in to the town.

There were no cars in front of the courthouse. I tethered my animal to a post at one of its corners and went up its steps. The doors were locked and I had to wait for the arrival of the custodian of the building. He looked like somebody's brother, nice but maybe a little violent underneath. Probably came from a family of thirteen kids and the mother and father had arguments every Saturday night. Why is it people always think of building custodians as being on the dumb and bumpkin side? We insist on believing in a lot of untrue things.

This custodian was too young to be settled in his kind of work. He said to me, "But there's nobody here yet. The offices won't be open for another hour. Why don't you go get yourself a cup of coffee and then come back? By that time I'll have the building warm."

I said, "No, I will just wait around here if you do not mind." We went in the building, and he went down some inside steps to a basement. I followed him and watched him build a fire in the big furnace there. He had red hair, and I asked him if he was any kin to the Luckabills at Pintail Fork. He considered. "I might be. Way back. You?"

I said, "No, I am one of the Lees from Blue Ash Hollow."

The custodian looked me over and this was not a rude or bold thing. I had on Holtie Petifer's surtout, which had suffered quite a bit since coming into my possession, and I had taken the scissors to my hair the night before; that is the only thing to do with hair after an illness; it is so lank. The custodian said, "You look like you come from a big family."

"No," I said, "there is just me. I am not really a kid in it either. I am the grandchild. Today I am bringing warrants against two daughters and one son of my grandparents for parent-neglect."

"I never heard of such a thing," commented the custodian. "It ought to be a good show with Judge Marriage presidin'. There's twelve kids in my family, not countin' myself. Say, is today Friday?"

"Yes, it is Friday."

"I knew it," said the custodian. "I always feel this way on Friday. Like I been hit by a road machine without knowin' it. Your folks ever fight?"

"No. They are too old for that now."

"Mine fight every Thursday night. Nobody gets any sleep."

"I had you pegged for coming from a family of Saturday-night fighters," I said, and after that the custodian and I were friends of a sort. We went back up the stairs to the main floor, and he showed me the "hearing room." "It's jerkwater, but the judge ain't. He talks straight, and you'll get justice."

I asked, "Where should I sit?" He led me down to a T-shaped table sitting on a little platform flanked on one side by the flag of the United States and on the other by that of the state of Arkansas. I chose a chair along the stem of the T and sat down and waited. The custodian left me, and I watched the clock on the wall.

At ten minutes to nine, Hutchens, Ora, Estie and a man I did not know arrived. They acted as if they did not know me and arranged themselves in chairs on the opposite side of the T-table. Hutchens wore a black topcoat, sniffled his catarrh and managed to look hang-dog. His friend kept talking to him in whispers and nodding to Ora and Estie and smiling at them. Estie held a handkerchief to her forehead and I was glad when, at two minutes after nine, Judge Marriage and a person I presumed to be an officer of the court marched in. The judge only faintly resembled the pasteboard man I had visited in the stone house in back of The Church of God. He had color in his face and purpose in his bearing. His white hair was brushed high. He took his seat at the end of the T-shaped table and looked around. He asked my relatives who they were, and they told him.

"Then you're the defendants in this case," said the judge.

"That is correct," said the little man with my relatives.

Judge Marriage glanced at me. "And you're Littabelle Lee, the plaintiff."

I said, "That is correct."

The officer of the court said, "Everybody raise his right hand. Do you-all swear to tell the truth, the whole truth and nothing but the truth?"

Everybody said yes. Judge Marriage then began to speak to us in a reasonable way, telling us what we were there for.

Immediately after Judge Marriage ceased speaking, the man with my aunts and uncle said, "Your honor, I move that this case be dismissed on the grounds that it is no case."

Judge Marriage locked his fingers and put them that way on his chin. The starch in his white shirtfront gleamed. He looked melancholy, like a wise baby. I thought he and the man knew each other from some time before this. "Counselor," he said, "I do not find that statement compelling. In fact, it don't catch my interest at all."

"I am up on my law," said the counselor. "And I must respectfully submit my opinion to you, sir, that you do not have a case to hear. The charge against my clients is parent-neglect, and to my knowledge that is not against any law in this state or any other state."

"To your knowledge," said Judge Marriage.

"Yes," affirmed the counselor. He had a neat face and an attractive voice. He had goat-eyes; I thought he might be well educated.

Judge Marriage regarded him tenderly, with sweet innocence. He said, "Well, maybe you're right. Maybe I don't have a case to hear, but since we're all here together like this, we might as well not waste the time. Let's just hear some about the trouble we're all here to try and straighten out, and then we'll decide whether we've got a case or not. Let's just hear from the plaintiff first."

I stood up and said, "I am Littabelle Lee, the plaintiff, your honor."

The judge looked away. I thought that might be his method for paying attention. He asked, "Is plaintiff represented by counsel?"

The custodian of the building was opening the double doors at the head of the hearing room and some people were filing in. I answered the judge. "No, sir. I am represented by myself. I represent my grandparents. They do not know anything about this though. Not yet."

"Tell us where you live," said Judge Marriage, still with his face averted.

"At Blue Ash Hollow."

"In a house?"

"No, in a barn."

"You and your grandparents live in a barn? Why?"

"Because our house burned down. It was hit by lightning last summer and burned to the ground."

"Does anybody else besides your grandparents live in your barn with you?"

"Sir?"

The judge swung around to look at me levelly. "I asked does anybody else live in your barn with you besides your grandparents."

"We have some chickens. They do."

"Who else?"

"Two hogs. My little burro. My grandpa's mule."

"I meant anybody human."

"Oh."

"Well, what's your answer?"

"Judge—"

"No, you are sworn to tell the truth. Now tell it. Does anybody else human besides your grandma and grandpa live in your barn with you?"

"I have an aunt. My aunt Sorrow. She is the one who raised me. The one who taught me everything I know. The one who has always taken care of me and Maw Maw and Paw Paw."

"She live in your barn with you?"

"Sir?"

"I said does your aunt Sorrow live in your barn with you?"

"Not now. She is gone."

"Gone where?"

"She had an accident. To her head. Now she is. . . . She is not right, and she has gone to live with. . . . She is married now to Mr. Winston Splitstone. They have a baby."

"What?" cried Estie, and Ora shrieked, "What?" and fell back in her chair, and Hutchens started to jump up, but was restrained by his lawyer. My three relatives stared at me, and the judge continued his questioning calmly, as if there had been no interruption in it.

"Do you have running water in your barn?"

"No. We carry our water from the creek."

"How do you see when it gets dark?"

"We use lanterns."

"I suppose you and your grandparents have enough to eat?"

"No, sir."

"Don't whisper. I can't hear you."

"No, sir. We do not have enough to eat. The fire burned up all the food we had laid by."

"I still can't hear you. Can't you speak up?"

"I SAID THE FIRE BURNED UP ALL THE FOOD WE HAD LAID BY. WE WILL PLANT NEW CROPS COME SPRING BUT NOW . . . NOW WE DO NOT HAVE ENOUGH TO EAT."

"Is your grandfather employed?"

"He farms some. He is too old to be employed."

Hutchens decided to cause a disturbance. He jumped to his feet and, throwing back the lapels of his coat, shouted, "Judge, that girl is makin' my sisters and I out to be monsters, and it just ain't so! The barn our parents is livin' in is more comfortable than any of our houses, and they've got a-plenty to eat! The land didn't burn down; it was just the house. And another thing. Holtie Petifer, their neighbor, is helpin' Paw Paw to raise a new house! It ain't as if they was going to have to live in the barn the rest of their lives!"

The judge did not reprimand Hutchens for his outburst. He said to Hutchens, "How old is your father?"

"He's up there," replied Hutchens, "but they ain't a thing in the world wrong with him. He's had it fat all these years. He don't have to worry about how he's going to meet his mortgage. He's got cash. Sorrow has always turned over what she makes from her practice to Paw Paw and Maw Maw."

"What practice is that?" inquired Judge Marriage, peering.

"Our sister Sorrow is a nature doctor and a midwife," said Hutchens.

"She has given that up," I said. "She is now married to Mr. Winston Splitstone, and they have a baby."

"That is disgraceful and ridiculous," said Ora. "If she had an accident to her head, it must have been a good one to make her want to run off and marry Winston Splitstone. And now a baby? Oh, dear Lord."

"I don't believe she had any accident to her head," said Estie spitefully. "She's always been flighty, and she's *always* wanted to marry Winston Splitstone."

Judge Marriage said, "All right, all right." Hutchens sat down. The judge asked me, "Are you employed?"

"I am deputy schoolkeeper at Pintail Fork. I got the job after I saved little Royce Fredericks' life. He lives at Pintail Fork and is fond of eating chalk. He got a piece stuck in his gullet the day I went and applied for the school-keeping job there and I cut a hole in his neck so he could breathe and that saved his life."

"Objection," said the counselor for Hutchens, Ora and Estie.

Judge Marriage swung his glance around to rest on the lawyer. "What objection?"

"The heroics of the plaintiff are irrelevant to this case," said the lawyer.

"You got a point," said Judge Marriage. To me he said, "Don't tell us about any more of your heroics. They're irrelevant to this case. What is your salary at Pintail Fork School?"

I told him, and he said, "And you and your grandparents live on that?"

"We are trying to. Three people cannot. One could, but not three. One of the troubles is, every time we go to the store for supplies we have to pay on an old debt, else the store owner will not sell to us. He is new here and does not know us yet. I had thought of buying what we need from the store at Pintail Fork, but the prices there are higher and it is a distance from there to Blue Ash Hollow and my only transportation is my little burro, Little Boy. Besides, that would not be fair, to take my trade to another store. I am not trying to avoid the debt."

"Any more troubles?" asked the judge.

"Yes, sir, a few. Skippers got to our meathouse, and we had to throw all of the meat in the creek. And our cows are lost. I think a coyote or wolves got them. Maw Maw lost her shoe, looking for them. And Paw Paw has the grippe. I doctored him with velvet dock leaves and sweetbrier hips. I thought if I could lay my hands on some good, red meat. . . . Well, I do not know. Two or three days ago I was in the woods and I saw a deer and I could have . . . could have killed him. . . . But I couldn't. . . . Pup was with me. . . . He's a little boy from Copsey Springs. . . . We are friends. . . . I *know* I can take care of my grandparents if only I could get a little temporary boost. . . . I have plans . . . I saw the deer. . . . we needed him to eat. . . . But I couldn't, I couldn't and now. . . . Well, I do not know. . . ."

The judge was pouring himself a glass of water from the pitcher on the table. He drank it and wiped his lips with a white handkerchief. The officer of the court was coming around the table to me, offering me his handkerchief. I took it and sat down. I blew my nose. Estie, Ora and Hutchens were staring at me. Their lawyer whispered to them. The spectators had been silent, but now they

began to talk among themselves. The little lawyer with
my relatives was arguing with them. All of a sudden he
made his move. He rose and said, "Your honor, I with-
draw from this case."

"Son," said Judge Marriage, "I wondered how long
it'd take you to get around to that. But, tell you what,
don't leave just yet. You might learn something. You defendants, you ever heard of the Decalogue, any of you?"

"No, I never heard of no Decalogue," said Ora.

"That's a list of laws pertaining to disrespect for parents, murder, theft, adultery, false accusations and so on,"
said Judge Marriage, "and they're punishable in most
legal systems of which we have knowledge."

Hutchens, Ora and Estie sat dumbfounded. Their little
lawyer was looking at the ceiling. Judge Marriage had
taken a watch from his vest-pocket and was looking at it.
"The time gets away, don't it? But all right, I think we
can wind this thing up now. You defendants, you got any
money with you?"

The defendants each drew back in their chairs. More
than ever the judge looked like a wise, melancholy baby,
leaning forward, white hair shining, his smile shining.
"Believe an old man. You'd be better off to pay."

"How much?" demanded Estie.

"How much you got with you?"

"Twenty dollars but I was saving it. . . . Oh, this is the
most humiliating thing. I never thought. . . . Well, you
just wait till I see Sorrow! You just wait!" She was crying
and rummaging through the contents of her purse.

"Bailiff," said Judge Marriage, and the bailiff jumped

smartly to the judge's side. The judge said, "Collect twenty dollars from each of these defendants and give 'em a receipt for it. Then you go to Blue Ash Hollow and turn it all over to the parents of these people. Tell 'em it's a present from their kids, and they can expect the same amount again on the first day of every month."

With her eyes gone wide, Estie said, "You mean that's your sentence? We got to pay twenty dollars every month to our parents?"

"You can mail it to the bailiff here," said Judge Marriage. "He's a friend of the court. Don't send no personal checks. Don't worry, you can trust him. I've known him since a week after he was born." The judge then rapped his mallet and that was all.

On the return trip to Blue Ash Hollow I had company. The bailiff from Judge Marriage's court rode beside me on his own mule. I said to him, "That lawyer for my uncle and aunts surprised me when he gave up like that."

Said the bailiff, "Oh, he knew he was riding a dead horse."

"Judge Marriage is a good man, isn't he?"

"The best."

"I think he has got a hard job. I think he must have a very big brain to do what he does. To know about the Decalogue and stuff like that."

"Oh," said the bailiff, "most everybody knows about the Decalogue. I think you do. You just don't know it by that name is all."

"What other name would I know it by?"

"The Decalogue," said the bailiff, "is the Ten Commandments. Given by God to Moses."

CHAPTER TWELVE

To describe Maw Maw's and Paw Paw's reactions to what I had done to my aunts and uncle I borrow a word from Winston Splitstone. Hoooeee! They were scandalized. They considered themselves to have been placed in public disgrace and humiliation and never mind my arguings for the necessity of the matter. Paw Paw said there was no necessity on earth big enough to make him favor such a devilish deed. He said were I not a young lady he would give me the whipping I deserved.

Maw Maw said I was not a true Lee, to have turned to such an act. For a while there was all billy-hell to pay.

Even during the sleep hours I would be awakened to hear the reproaches, spoken harshly in the darkness. Finally I took my blankets to the lower part of the barn and slept with the animals. In his burro dreams, Little Boy snorted and kicked.

I was commanded to write lengthy letters to Hutchens, Ora and Estie, explaining Maw Maw's and Paw Paw's innocence in the matter and make apology for my own part in it. Those three shitepokes must have put their heads together before sitting down to construct their answers. All said they had never thought Maw Maw and Paw Paw to be guilty, but that apology could mend none of it. Said what was done was done. Ora said she would pray for me.

Estie said it was beyond her imagination to think she owed anything to Maw Maw and Paw Paw. It had not been her idea to come into the world and her childhood had been a wretched one. Due to her lack of education, she had been forced to marry a man old enough to be her father and not anybody knew what she suffered. Her life with Tilman Spanhank was just too wet to plow. Now hovering close to senility, he spent all of his silly days ogling their young girl roomers, chasing them up and down the stairs, cavorting with them on the porches. It was sickening and mortifying. Florine, the daughter, could not have any friends because of Tilman. The poor child cried herself to sleep almost every night, and there was not a thing she, Estie, could do about it. She did not know how she was going to manage to send twenty dollars a month to Maw Maw and Paw Paw. Still, she did not have the time to sit in jail. I was a wicked girl and she, also, would pray for me.

Hutchens said on account of the obligation imposed by me through Judge Marriage, he and Mispah were having to think of new, drastic ways to make ends meet. Mispah had discharged their laundress and he, Hutchens, had given up cigars. He said he would send his money every month but not for us to look for a visit from him any time soon. He would be glad when I got married, he said, and changed my name to another. I was not a Lee and did not deserve the use of the name. He wished me luck.

I showed those letters to Winston Splitstone. "Maybe Hutchens and Maw Maw are right. Maybe I am not a Lee and never have been."

"There might could be two ways you could look at that," said The Hermit. "You're a Lee all right, but you're a good deal like your mother too. I remember her. She was never satisfied with the way things was but always had to be changing them around, trying to better them." It was a day in January and we were sitting on his stoop. The cold sunshine was dry and brilliant. The Hermit held the drowsing baby, Ward, who roused every once in a while to crane a stern look at me.

"He still does not trust me," I said. "Isn't that funny? If it wasn't for me, maybe he wouldn't be here. That's some gratitude for you."

"Gratitude is not a very popular virtue," commented Winston Splitstone. "The older you get the more you'll find that out."

"I might leave this place," I said.

"Aw now," said Mr. Splitstone, "your folks aren't a-gonna stay mad at you forever. Personally I think they ought to be grateful to you, but maybe their minds can't work in that direction just now. Maybe I did wrong in steering you to go to Judge Marriage. I might should have told you any time you go between parents and their kids you can look for some ugly feelings to come from either one side or the other. Sometimes both."

"I think I might be finished here for a while," I said. "You wouldn't happen to know who invented scissors, would you?"

The Hermit considered. "I'm afraid not. That's one question just never came to my mind."

"How about shoestrings?"

"I'm afraid I never thought much about that either. Littabelle, you lettin' them kids of yours drive you crazy?"

"I don't think so. I think we are driving each other that way with what we don't know. Mr. Splitstone, do you think the world will ever sink?"

"Sink? Sink where?"

"That is what I am asking you. If the world ever gets too many people in it, too much weight, will it sink? Where will it go? Oh, I wish I knew the answers to things, but I don't so I cannot teach them. Oh, I wish I could go away and learn to be a real teacher. Mr. Splitstone, do you remember a governor of this state ever coming to Blue Ash Hollow?"

"Sure," replied Winston Splitstone. "It was a long time ago, but I remember it. Came here to hunt. He put on some show for us. He and his party pitched camp right above your Paw Paw's place, and after they'd been there about three days the governor got sick. Sorrow said he must have eaten some kind of poison berries. Anyway he turned greener than any grass you ever saw. Swelled up like a balloon. We all thought he was going to die. Well, there wasn't any medical doctor and he was so bad off he couldn't be moved so Sorrow went up there and she saved him."

I said, "I do not remember that."

"Oh," said Winston Splitstone, "You was just a little kid then."

"Where do you think that man is now?"

"That governor? Well, he's not governor anymore, but he's still a high up muckety-muck in Little Rock. Every time I get a chance to see a newspaper, I see his name in it. Every once in a while Sorrow talks about going down there and collecting the favor he owes her."

I said, "Maybe she would not mind if I went down and collected it for her," but Winston Splitstone did not hear me. The baby, Ward, was letting it be known he was tired of sitting in the sun and might be hungry.

Hoooeee, that is the way great ideas are born. The more I thought about it, the better it looked. I could draw the picture of this rambunctious proceeding in my mind. Me and Little Boy riding into the ex-governor's town one fine summer day. The governor's grand house. The governor would look something like Judge Marriage, and his wife would be there. She would invite me to sit in the shade on her porch, and the three of us would eat raisin cake and drink cold drinks and I would tell them about my school and the children at Pintail Fork and about myself. *Governor, I am here to ask your advice and maybe I need a little bit more than that too. I can teach; that is what I want to do. I have found that out. But there is a limit to what a person like me can do; I have found that out too. So I need to go for a while to the place where teachers are taught how to be teachers and learn to be a real one. You remember that time my Aunt Sorrow saved your life, sir?*

When you want something or need something bad enough, you will cut any corner. There is nothing wrong with that providing you act in a good cause and are not governed only by self-interest.

In March of that year the usual cold, stinging winds of that month raided us, and then we had days of rain and Paw Paw and Holtie Petifer grumbled that they could not get out and work in the fields and on the new log house which, by that time, was near to completion.

Spring was late. It did not come until the first week in April, flushing up from the south, creeping up and over our hills and down into our hollows in a warming, light-green tide.

In May I said to myself—Everything is all right here now for a while, at least. When school lets out, I will go. One night I stood in the doorway of the lower half of our barn, thinking that. The moon was rising from behind the hills; my owl in his tree across the creek was laughing.

The light from the moon flowed upward and I saw a shooting star, streaking from the northeast, blazing a swift, fiery trail. I wondered where it would land.